THE PERIL AHEAD

THE DEPARTMENT Z SERIES

The Death Miser

Redhead

First Came a Murder

Death Round the Corner

The Mark of the Crescent

Thunder in Europe

The Terror Trap

Carriers of Death

Days of Danger

Death Stands By

Menace

Murder Must Wait

Panic!

Death by Night

The Island of Peril

Sabotage

Go Away Death

The Day of Disaster

Prepare for Action

No Darker Crime

Dark Peril

The Peril Ahead

The League of Dark Men

The Department of Death

The Enemy Within

Dead or Alive

A Kind of Prisoner

The Black Spiders

THE PERIL AHEAD
DEPARTMENT Z

JOHN CREASEY

OPEN ROAD
INTEGRATED MEDIA
NEW YORK

ISBN: 978-1-5040-9220-3

This edition published in 2024 by Open Road Integrated Media, Inc.
180 Maiden Lane
New York, NY 10038
www.openroadmedia.com

THE PERIL AHEAD

1

THE GENIUS OF GABRIEL TOLLER

They say,' said a vacuous-looking young man dressed in white flannels, an old jacket, and a sweater in which some loving hand had prettily weaved strands of red and blue, 'that the old chap in the corner was nearly murdered *nine times* up to the end of last year.' The young man spoke in a hushed voice and peered as if with short-sighted eyes at his companion; he was pleading to be believed.

'And he doesn't look a bit like a cat,' said Polly Dalton, keeping a straight face. That was difficult, because her lips liked to smile, and when they did, dimples in her plump cheeks were born anew and laughter shone in her blue eyes.

'A *cat?*' echoed the vacuous but earnest young man. Polly did not help him out. 'Cat,' repeated the young man, and then understanding dawned upon him. 'Oh, a *cat!* Nine lives! Oh, by Jove, jolly good! I say, marvellous!'

'I'm glad you like it,' murmured Polly, and for once the dimples were not brought to life, because the spindly youth embarrassed her. His large, horn-rimmed glasses made him look in the early twenties, but his behaviour was that of a youth in the early teens.

Polly Dalton wondered how she could get away from him.

In front of them, on the table in the open lounge of the *Mayberry Hotel*, were tankards of cider. Polly was dressed in a cream shirt-blouse and a cream pleated skirt which did not reach her dimpled knees, ankle socks which made her firm, round legs look very plump, and tennis shoes. By the side of her wicker chair was her tennis racquet. She was pleasantly tired after three sets with the spindly youth, whose name she did not know.

After lunch she had looked round the small dining-room and asked: 'Would anyone care for some tennis?' The youth had been the only one to say 'yes'. She had seen him at breakfast, and felt sorry for him, he looked so woebegone and helpless. She had expected no pleasure from a game of pat-ball, but found the youth transformed on the court. He performed prodigies of recovery, and as they had walked to the lounge she had an uncomfortable feeling that he had let her win. Then she had allowed herself to admit that she had nothing to do for the rest of the afternoon, and so was fated to have him as a companion at least until tea-time.

'I *do* like a good joke,' he said, three minutes after he had stopped laughing. Then he grew serious again. 'It's a fact, though, Miss Dalton. Nine times! He's a *genius*.'

'At avoiding being murdered, you mean,' said Polly, for she had a fair wit.

'I *say*,' said her companion, doubled up again, 'you *are* good, you know! You really are! By Jove, marvellous! I wish I could think of something clever to say sometimes.'

'I'm sure you can, sometimes,' said Polly, her distress growing deeper. He would soon become maudlin. 'How did you know my name?'

'Oh, that was easy,' said the young man, beaming. 'It's on a tag on your ball net. I say, would you mind very much—I mean—curiosity and all that—er—what does the E stand for?'

He meant the 'E' which came before Dalton on the telltale label, and Polly, casting almost desperate glances about the room, said that it stood for Ethel but that her friends called her Polly. The young man asked whether they did, really. Then he hesitated as if he were about to ask humbly whether he might join the circle of her friends, but surprisingly conquered the impulse and volunteered the information that his name was George.

'George,' he repeated, his eyes bright behind the clear lenses, 'George!' He beamed. 'You didn't expect that, did you?'

'Er—what?' asked Polly, distractedly.

'George, George,' said George, and slapped his bony knees. 'Ha-ha-ha! It surprises everyone. As a matter of fact,' he added, suddenly sober, 'I've a middle name. I don't tell everyone that, it rather spoils the joke, doesn't it? But I don't mind telling you. It's Henry.'

'Oh,' said Polly, blankly.

'George, Henry, George,' declared George, and added anxiously: 'You do see, don't you? Christian names George Henry, surname just George.'

Polly clutched her tankard.

'What, no hyphen?' she said, and plunged her face towards the cider. She kept it there until George Henry George had recovered from the exquisite witticism, and then found herself looking at a slim, gold cigarette-case extended towards her. She could not help noticing his fingers and the perfect filbert shape of the nails; his hands were perfectly kept.

'Thank you,' she said.

George lit the cigarettes from a gold lighter, and tucked

both case and lighter beneath his sweater, revealing for a moment a pale blue silk singlet.

'No,' he said, 'he certainly doesn't look like a cat. True.' Incredibly, he was serious. 'A lion, now.'

'Do lions go white?' asked Polly, with difficulty.

The remark did not occasion another outburst of astonished applause; George continued to be serious.

'Well, I've never seen an old lion,' he said, 'so far as I know. I mean, that great massive head and beard—patriarchal, isn't it? He's a marvellous old boy!'

'Really,' said Polly.'

'Oh, I know what I'm talking about,' said George, very earnestly. 'I know a man who knows him jolly well. He's a genius. Not my friend,' he hastened to make clear, 'the old gentleman in the corner. Mind you, my friend's very clever, too. But I don't think he would call himself a genius. Not quite.' He glanced towards the corner, and then turned hastily away, for the old gentleman with the massive head and the magnificent spade-shaped beard—which was as white as his luxuriant hair—was looking towards him. 'Don't look!' he warned, urgently. 'He's staring at us. Perhaps he knows we're talking about him.'

'We mustn't embarrass him,' said Polly, clutching her racquet. 'And I *ought* to go up to my room and write some letters.'

'Oh, I *say!*' said George, in acute disappointment. 'Wouldn't a card do? If you haven't any cards,' he added, leaning forward confidentially, 'I could give you one or two funny ones. *Do* make a card do.'

'I really can't,' said Polly; 'it's to my mother—and my sister and some old friends,' she added, recklessly. 'I ought not to have played tennis this afternoon, thank you *so* much for the game!' She collected her racquet and bag, gave George a quick, dimpling smile, and fled.

He stared disconsolately after her.

The Mayberry Hotel was a small private hotel in Bournemouth, close to the sea and almost abutting the edge of the cliffs. Among its attractions was a tennis court, the one thing which had decided Polly Dalton in its favour. She had hoped, however, for a crowd of young people, but George Henry George was the only one whom she had met. That morning she had caught a glimpse of a harassed young woman putting a baby into a pram in the garden, with another child, no more than two years old, clinging to her skirts, but for the rest the residents were old or middle-aged.

As she sat down at her dressing-table and began to write her letters—a duty which she had earlier decided to defer until the next day, but was far better than bearing with the crashing bore—she found herself thinking of the 'genius'. He looked eighty if he were a day. She had almost cannoned into him when she had come from the bathroom that morning, and noticed his remarkably handsome features, his clear, white skin—almost transparent and seeming to glow—and his clear grey eyes. He had impressed her then, and George's remarks heightened her interest. *Had* the old man really been attacked? *Had* he narrowly escaped being murdered? Was he a genius? If so, what did he do?

Curiously enough, she could not get George's earnest face out of her mind's eye. He had remarkable eyes as well as fine hands. Once or twice she had found herself wondering whether he really needed the glasses or whether they were an affectation. She tried to remember when he had looked at her ball-bag. The label was an old one, and the ink was faded; only someone with good eyes could have made out the name at a glance. She was quite sure that he had not picked the bag up and examined it closely.

'...the position is glorious, and it's a perfect day. Looking across the bay—the Mayberry is on the East Cliff, and you can see across to a place called Studland, near Swanage, I think—it's a dream picture. The cliff walks are lovely. I'm told that a feature of the town are the chines, wooded valleys leading down to the sea...'

A sound made her turn her head. It seemed to come from the passage, a curious scratching noise. It stopped, then started again, and continued at brief intervals.

'Is anyone there?' she called.

There was no answer, but the scratching noise ceased abruptly. She got up and went to the door. No one was in the passage, but she heard a movement and a sound, as if one of the nearby doors had been closed. Frowning, she went back to the dressing-table.

'...and so I had a stroke of good fortune [she continued]. *The room reserved for me wasn't free, after all, the man who had it before me is staying on, and I've been given a double room, with marvellous views of the bay. I'm next door to a remarkable old man with a snow-white beard, the very image of an Old Testament Prophet as portrayed on Sunday School walls....'*

She broke off, this time with an exclamation of annoyance, for the scratching noise had started again. She sat quite still, looking at the reflection of the door in the mirror. She had an uneasy fancy that someone was trying to get into the room, undetected, but the handle was not moving. There was no need to use a tool, anyway, because the door was not locked.

The sound continued. It was rather like a mouse scratching in the wall.

She pushed the stool back firmly, not quite able to understand why she was so affected. The touch of mystery about it intrigued her, and she dismissed the idea that it was a mouse. She tip-toed towards the door, but when she was only half-way across the room there was a tap *at the window*.

She swung round.

By the window, peering in at her and displaying his wide, foolish grin, was George Henry George. He was beckoning her and making hideous faces, as if to reassure her. She felt furiously angry, and strode across the room. One window was wide open, but the other was closed, because a stiff breeze was coming off the sea. George was by the closed one. As she drew nearer, he put a hand to his mouth and pursed his lips and tapped them, enjoining her to silence.

Then her heart nearly turned over, for George slipped.

One moment he was standing with his head and shoulders and one arm in full view, the next he had disappeared. There was a tearing sound, but no cry of alarm or distress. She saw a hand wave wildly, and then clutch the window-sill. By the time she reached the window and opened it, George was climbing back on some creeper, pulling himself up with one arm. Now she could see that he had climbed from a small balcony in the room next to hers—not the old man's room—and his feet were on the ledge which surrounded the balcony.

'What do you mean—' she began, between alarm and anger.

'*Hush-shush-shush!*' hissed George. His glasses had become unlodged in his fall and were hanging on to one ear. For the first time she noticed that his ears were small and pale, rather attractive, like his hands. '*Oh, hush-shush-shush!*' repeated George, urgently.

Tight-lipped, she rescued his glasses, then gripped his wrist and pulled. He scrambled over the window-sill, making little sound. One moment she had his wrist in her fingers, the next the hold had been shifted and he was gripping hers.

'Polly the Powerful,' he said, making her gasp. 'Silence was never more golden. All will be explained.' He adjusted his glasses, and grinned vacantly at her—but *was* the grin so vacant?

'If I were a giraffe, this wouldn't be necessary,' George went on brightly. 'Enormous advantages giraffes have over human beings. First floor windows are never safe from them! Have you heard anything odd?'

'Heard?' she echoed, faintly.

'Noises,' said George. 'I—*oh, hush, shush-shush!*' He looked positively panic-stricken and stared towards the door, but his grip on her arm did not slacken.

The scratching noise, which had either ceased or had been drowned by their movements and whispered words, started afresh. George kept quite still for several seconds, then released her wrist and patted her forearm.

'Good girl,' he said. 'Reliable in a crisis. Bless you.' He stepped towards the door with his long, springy stride, which somehow failed to be ungainly. He opened the door slowly, making no sound. He peered into the passage, without putting his head through the doorway, then nearly closed the door and beckoned her, putting his fingers to his lips as he finished. Completely bewildered, she joined him. As she looked into the passage she saw the back of a man who was standing outside the door of the Old Testament Prophet.

'Tenth attempt on Gabriel,' said George, closing the door without making a sound. 'Not the angel, the genius. Gabriel Toller, a shining light of the twentieth century. Can you act?'

'What *are* you drivelling about?' she demanded, but she kept her voice low. 'No, I can't act.'

'Be brave,' he urged. 'Try. Go to the middle of the room, push a chair to one side, utter an explosive *"damn!"* and after a pause add: *"Ink!"* Having done that, walk heavily but not quickly to the door. Go into the passage, closing door firmly behind you, and then hurry down to the lounge. Oh—on entering the passage, be tight-lipped and show exasperation, as with me downstairs. Remember?'

'Why should I do anything of the kind?' she demanded.

He pulled up his sweater, gay with its red and blue, showed his blue silk singlet for a moment, and, as if by sleight of hand, drew a card from beneath it. 'As rabbits from hats,' he said, and handed it to her with a flourish.

He looked at her steadily. Fool that he was, there was gravity in his expression. She read the card, and could not believe what was written there. She stared at him, astonished, then looked at the card again. It was printed: *'Metropolitan Police, Criminal Investigation Department, New Scotland Yard, S.W.1,'* and on one side was a small photograph, unmistakably a likeness of George. Beneath the heading was a request to all civil authorities to render the bearer, George Henry George, all necessary assistance. Beneath that were two signatures, with a line of print beneath them. The first signature was unreadable, and the print said: *'Home Secretary.'* The second signature was very clear: *'Archibald Chatworth, Assistant Commissioner.'*

That was not all.

In faint print was a capital 'Z' over which everything was superimposed.

'Become a civil authority for a moment,' urged George. 'Please!' He smiled at her, winningly.

She was as quick at making up her mind as she was at

retort. After a prolonged stare at him, she turned away, pulled a chair towards her so that it made considerable noise, and then exclaimed aloud: *'Damn, the ink's run out!'*

At the first sound, the scratching stopped.

She paused, and then added, in a quieter voice:

'I suppose there'll be some downstairs.' She walked steadily towards the door, and glanced at George, who was standing and clapping his hands together, making no sound, but grinning at her delightedly. *'Fool!'* she hissed, and opened the door.

2
GEORGE HENRY'S BLACK EYE

A door closed farther along the passage.

Polly looked towards the old man's room, but no one was standing outside it now. She hesitated only for a moment, then walked towards the head of the stairs. There were only four rooms in the passage, for the room with the balcony from which George had come was entered from the landing.

Polly disappeared.

Almost against her will, she started to go downstairs, but she wanted to see what happened in the passage, and halfway down she hesitated....

The young man with the vacuous expression half expected that, but he thought the girl would have enough wit to realize that she must do no more than peer round the corner, and he hoped that the man trying to break into Gabriel Toller's room would not notice her. He himself had seen the man at work fifteen minutes before, and there was a reasonable chance that he had the lock almost back; any man worth his salt as a cracksman could have done it in three minutes.

George stood near the door, listening.

The scratching sound came again, but suddenly stopped, and a faint sigh followed, probably one of satisfaction. A door squeaked.

'And not a drop of oil,' said George, *sotto voce*. 'Save me from amateurs!'

The door squeaked again, presumably as it closed, and by that time George was standing in the passage. He heard the bolt shot home, and a broad grin made his mouth stretch almost from ear to ear. He stepped to Gabriel Toller's door and waited for perhaps two minutes. Then he turned and looked along the passage—and he saw Polly Dalton's fair, curly hair, and her rounded eyes. He waved her away, and she disappeared. He grinned again, then stood in front of the door with his right shoulder towards it, and thrust his shoulder forward.

It looked incredibly simple. The door burst open, with hardly any effort, and George stepped calmly into the room. Earlier that day, with Toller's consent, he had loosened the screws of the bolt.

Standing by the bed, looking over his shoulder and with something in his right hand, was a short, plump man—much plumper than Polly. He was dressed in an immaculate suit of grey flannel. He was not a bad-looking man, but he looked absurd with his mouth open and his eyes almost popping out of his head in surprise.

'Not this time, Marmaduke,' said George.

'Marmaduke' swung round. The thing in his right hand sailed through the air towards George, who caught it neatly and dropped it into his pocket as he moved. The fat man backed towards the window. His left hand was in the air, as if in a gesture of surrender, but his right went into his pocket.

'Silly fellow,' said George.

14

He drove his left fist towards the man's stomach. The fat man snatched his hand from his pocket to fend off the blow, and left his chin wide open. George struck him with a right swing, intending that swing to finish the fat man's immediate interest in life. He was disagreeably surprised by the way the man swayed back on his feet. The punch landed too far forward, and George, who had put all his power into it, nearly lost his balance. A fist like a ham struck him in the eye and sent him reeling back. The fat man backed away and put his right hand to his pocket again, taking his time over it....

Polly Dalton, unable to restrain her curiosity, reached the open doorway of the room. She saw George backing towards her, trying to regain his balance, and the fat man glaring at George. *In the fat man's hand was an automatic.*

Polly screamed.

The fat man started and turned startled eyes towards her, and in that moment George, recovering, launched himself bodily at his adversary. There was one shot, a barking sound, a faint yellow flash, which Polly heard and saw as she stood still, unable to speak or move after that one high-pitched cry. Then George reached the man, and the gun went flying to the bed, there was a flurry of arms and hands, and a series of squelching noises. She had never seen anything like it. Fury unleashed sprang from George Henry George, and in two minutes the fat man, his face battered, blood coming from his lips and one eye, was on the floor beneath the window. He was sobbing for breath, but still trying to fend his assailant off.

Footsteps were sounding on the stairs.

'Shut the door!' hissed George. 'Tell 'em you saw a mouse. Hurry!' He looked at her out of one eye, for the other was closed, red and swollen. His words broke through the paralysis which had gripped her, and she obeyed automatically. George heard her say 'mouse', and there was a medley of voices, men's and women's one against another. George stepped to the door and put a chair beneath the handle, in case anyone showed too much curiosity. Then he returned to his victim, who was gasping for breath and trying to get to his feet.

'Sit against the wall,' said George, softly, and the man obeyed.

'Stay there,' ordered George, and the man showed no inclination to move. 'There's a good boy,' said George.

He picked the gun up from the bed, looked at it, put the safety-catch on, and slipped it into his pocket. It knocked against the missile, which he took out and looked at thoughtfully. It was a small tin, about the size of a twenty cigarette packet, and was quite heavy. He held it to his ear, and heard a faint ticking sound.

'Set for midnight, or thereabouts,' he said aloud. 'You are not original.'

The fat man did not speak.

'Get up and wash yourself,' said George. 'I can't take you through the streets like that.'

The man dragged himself to his feet. His face was a mass of bruises, and one eye was as swollen as George's. His lip was cut and still bleeding, and blood was splashed on his shirt, collar and coat. He winced when he saw himself in the mirror, but he ran cold water in the hand-basin, and began to bathe his face. George watched him thoughtfully. The voices outside had stopped, but he did not think he would be left in peace for long.

The fat man was only half-way through his unexpected ablutions when there was a light but very firm tap at the door.

'Who's that?' inquired George, softly.

'It's me,' said Polly Dalton. 'If you don't let me in, I shall—'

'Now would I keep you out?' asked George. He took the chair away and opened the door, greeting Polly with a broad smile, which was now one-sided, for the swelling at his eye had spread to his cheek.

She looked at him in some concern.

'Your eye,' she said.

'You ought to see the other fellow's,' said George, and then he touched her arm and added, lightly but with obvious seriousness: 'If you hadn't come, I would be dead meat, and for that I shall reward you with a most unbelievable true story, but not just now. Will you go downstairs, telephone Bournemouth 81818 and, when a man answers you—and a man will—just ask him to send a taxi along to the *Mayberry Hotel.* Is that clear?'

'I thought you were a policeman,' she said. 'Why don't you telephone the police?'

'Of questions and answers you will have your fill later,' said George. 'Mystery will be unravelled, and a first-class reference obtained as to the character of George Henry George. I feel that perhaps I might be wise, at this point, to exhort you to use the utmost discretion, to discuss this adventure with no one, and, when you see me later with my eye nicely blackened and ripe, I hope you will express maidenly surprise and deep feminine concern.'

'I won't natter about it,' said Polly, and went to the door from where she flung at him an ominous: 'Yet.' George rubbed his chin and smiled, and then paid more attention to the fat man.

His victim had dried himself on a towel, but his lip was still bleeding, and so was the cut over his eye. He stood by the wash-basin, leaning heavily against it, completely defeated and spiritless. George looked at him steadily, and the fat man shifted his gaze.

'Name, please,' said George.

'I—look here,' the man said, with an effort, 'I don't know what was in that packet, I was asked to put it in the old boy's bed—it's a joke, see.' When George did not immediately express scepticism, the fat man continued with newfound enthusiasm: 'It was just a joke so far as I was concerned, like making an apple-pie bed.' He received no spoken discouragement, and went on desperately: 'You often make up apple-pie beds at hotels like this—'

'Not in Bournemouth!' exclaimed George. 'My dear chap, have regard for the proprieties! You can do things like that in Blackpool, Margate and Southend-on-Sea, but not in Bournemouth. The argument just won't carry.'

The fat man fell silent.

'Name, please,' said George.

'My—my name's Smith.'

'Oh, Smith,' said George, stepping to the other's side. 'Smith' backed away, and even tried to defend himself, but in a few seconds he was spun round on his feet and George had one sleeve of his coat free; he completed disrobing the man with astonishing speed, as if it were a kind of sleight of hand, and then retired to the bed with his trophy. The sleeves of the coat were inside out, and the inside breast pocket was revealed, showing a fat wallet.

George emptied the contents on the bed, and examined a card with great interest, narrowing his one usable eye. 'Percival Algernon Merryweather. Ugh!'

Letters in the wallet were addressed to P. A. Merryweather, Esq., at a variety of addresses. Among the other contents were several five-pound notes, a large number of one-pound notes, postage stamps and visiting-cards in other names—but only one in each name.

Merryweather watched all this without protest.

'So your name is Merryweather, Apple-Pie,' mused George. 'It doesn't suit you. I now invite you to tell me why you came to Professor Toller's room and tried to plant an infernal machine in his bed.'

'It's *not* an infernal machine!' cried Merryweather. 'It was a joke, that's all; just a joke!'

'Too bad,' said George. 'It misfired, and I can sympathize with you—mine often do. The prisoner refused to make a statement,' he added, looking into the mirror, 'and he was therefore delivered, sound in wind and limb, slightly damaged in face and spirit, to a certain section of the Special Branch, with the request: "Please open the gentleman's mouth, method unimportant".'

As he spoke there was another tap at the door, quiet but firm, as before. He called out, and Polly answered him; promptly he invited her in.

'They're sending a cab at once,' she said.

'Splendid!' cried George. 'Always at our service. Miss Dalton, you've done so much that I hesitate to ask for more, but duty calls. No, nothing very much,' he added, hastily, 'and I will tell you the whole story—item as earnest. Apple-Pie's name is Merryweather.' He pointed at the fat man, and Polly let his inanity pass. 'Two small things,' he said. 'First, go to my room and get my hat. My largest hat, so that I can pull the brim over my damaged eye. Nothing will hide the damage to Apple-Pie's fair countenance, but that doesn't matter much. Having brought the said hat to me, go downstairs and wait for the taxi. Have you been in Bournemouth long?'

'No,' said Polly, faintly.

'Then I will describe to you the taxis of Bournemouth,' said George. 'They are in two categories, the opulent and ostentatious, or the fine old vintage, Daimler or Rolls-Royce about 50 B.C. The driver of this one will be in ordinary clothes, a handsome man, a man who has a penchant for pretty lassies and will not be above ogling you. Return his gaze coldly. Ask him to wait, and then come and tell me he's waiting. There's a real pet,' he added, and grinned so engagingly that she uttered a short, half-indignant laugh, and asked him his room number.

'Number 11,' said George. 'Second floor. Catch.' He took a key from beneath his sweater and pretended to throw it. By the time she had finished trying to catch it, he was at her side and pressing it into her hand. 'It'll be worth it,' he said, soothingly, 'and not all my friends are like me.'

'Too *bad*!' said Polly.

'Retorts falling off in quality,' murmured George, and smiled when she went out.

He sat on the end of the bed, looking at his prisoner from his one eye. The other was more swollen and was extremely painful, a fact which obtruded on his thoughts. There were other, more important, intrusions. He was uneasy at the part which Polly Dalton had played. Before long he would probably be strongly reprimanded for having induced her to help him, but there had been no obvious way in which to avoid it. He watched Merryweather closely, and now and again he got up and looked out of the window. After a while, he said: 'Can't she find that hat?'

Polly Dalton, half-amused and half-angry, but rather more amused than angry as well as greatly puzzled, went upstairs and found that the second floor was similar to the first, with which she was now familiar. It did not occur to her that Room 11 was immediately above Room 5, which was then occupied by George and his companion. The more she thought of what had happened, the more bewildered she felt, and she did not give her mind to turning the key in the lock. She fiddled for a few seconds, and then muttered an expletive, and said: 'It *can't* be the wrong key.'

It was not. When she inserted the key properly, the lock turned smoothly, and she stepped into the room. It was in some confusion—the room, she thought, of a man who did not know the meaning of tidiness. She saw that a drawer was nearly out of the dressing-table, and the contents were strewn on the floor. She frowned, and then espied a trilby hat, which was hanging on the corner of the single bed.

She turned to get it, and as she did so a man stepped from behind the door and covered her mouth with his hand.

3

HAND OVER MOUTH

It was a large, powerful hand. It smacked against Polly's face and smothered her cry. The thumb on one side of her jaw and the forefinger on the other pressed so hard that her bones seemed about to crack. The pain was agonizing. She felt herself going faint, hot tears sprang to her eyes. Her feet seemed to float in the air, and her head was pressed back, causing a red-hot pain at the back of her neck.

She thought her neck would break.

Then, only slowly at first, the grip relaxed. The man pulled her head forward. The pain was no less, but the strain eased. As slowly he eased off the pressure of his thumb and forefinger. Her cheeks seemed to swell, and her throat felt swollen; she could breathe only through her nose, and with difficulty.

Then he pushed her head forward, using his other hand with the fingers spaced over her cranium. He turned her round at the same time, so that she was looking into the mirror. She saw the reflection of the man and herself. Then he pushed her head between her knees, and she was unable to help herself.

When he let her straighten up, still keeping his hand on her head, she was dizzy but the pain had eased, and in a few seconds she could see his reflection clearly. He was not much taller than she, but a broad-shouldered, powerful man. His face was set, the mouth very straight—a face which was not quite human. His skin was rough and red, and not natural, but his eyes, deep-set and very bright, were full of life. He was dressed in dark grey, which threw her cream clothes and pink flesh into sharp relief. She was trembling from head to foot; the pleated skirt danced up and down just above her knees.

'What happened downstairs?' he demanded, and pressed his fingers into her scalp, so that she felt pain again, as well as the tenderness about her neck and ears.

'N-n-nothing!' she gasped.

The way he could hurt her, without appearing to move his hands, was terrifying. She had gone red after the shock, but now the colour drained away from her face.

'Did George catch anyone?' he demanded, maintaining the tighter pressure and pushing her head forward.

'Y-yes!' she gasped. 'Yes!'

'Are they still downstairs?'

She was surprised that in spite of her fear of the man and of the pain he could cause, she could still think clearly. She screwed up her face, as if the pain were unbearable, and answered in an agonized voice:

'He took him away in a taxi.'

'That's a lie,' said the man.

'It isn't a lie, I rang for the taxi myself!'

'What number?' he demanded.

'I don't remember! It was—' She caught a mind picture of a small car with a name written on it, the taxi which had brought her from the station. 'It was Autax, or something like that. Auto, Autax!'

His grip relaxed a little, and she knew that he was inclined to believe her. He stared into the mirror for a moment, and then said, thoughtfully:

'So he took him away in an ordinary cab, did he? What address did he give?'

'I don't know, he wouldn't let me go with him, he hurried downstairs with the man as soon as the taxi arrived.' Her mind was much clearer, and she could elaborate without difficulty. 'He asked me to come up here.'

'Why?' demanded the man.

She was ready for that.

'I told him I would go to the police unless he told me what it was all about, and he gave me a key and asked me to wait up here for him.'

'Did he?' said the man. He seemed in two minds whether to believe that or not. 'What else happened?'

She told him a garbled story of what had transpired downstairs, without mentioning the name of Gabriel Toller or going into any other details. He seemed satisfied. He also seemed confident of himself, and by now she was worried in case George Henry George came up to find out what was detaining her. If he walked into the room without a thought of danger, this man would be more than a match for him.

The man was looking into the mirror where he could see her and the door, and he was staring at the door as he asked:

'You knew him before you arrived here, didn't you?'

'No, I came for a holiday.'

He pushed her head forward. 'You knew him. Don't tell me lies!'

'It isn't true,' she gasped. 'I came here for a holiday. I played tennis with him this afternoon, that's all.'

She saw his eyes glint, but broke off when he pushed her forward roughly, and let her go. She came up against the dressing-table and bumped her nose against the mirror, not knowing what had made him thrust her away from him. She sensed that he turned round.

She did not see him drop his hand to his pocket, nor see the door burst open.

George came in, at first upright and moving very fast; then he launched himself forward in a flying tackle. He got a grip of the man's ankles before the other could get out his gun, and brought him down with a crash that shook the room. The man's elbow cracked into the small of Polly's back as she was trying to recover her balance, and she slumped forward again, unable to repress a cry of pain. She was aware of sundry noises, gasping and grunting, sharper sounds when everything was knocked off the dressing-table, a crash when a glass broke. She dragged herself towards the window, and sat helplessly against the wall. She was just in time to see the broad-shouldered man pick up a chair and swing it at George, and this time she screamed in real earnest.

George side-stepped.

The broad-shouldered man let go of the chair, and for a moment it was mixed up with George's long arms. The other made a bee-line for the door. There were people in the passage, and she heard cries of alarm and a thud. Someone fell just outside the room. There were heavy footsteps on the stairs.

George Henry George finished juggling with the chair, put it down gently, and said quite clearly:

'Oh, dear, he's got away.'

He did not go to the door, nor trouble about the people who suddenly burst into the room, but turned to Polly and gave her a most engaging smile. He bent down and put his hands beneath her elbows, and in a moment she was on her feet. It seemed no effort for him to lift her. She swayed, and he gripped her waist, lifted her clear of the floor and carried her to the easy-chair in one corner, heavy though she was. He put her into it, and stood back.

'No bones broken, I hope,' he said.

'I don't think so,' muttered Polly.

'Good girl! I shall stand you the largest dinner you have had in your life for this!'

He turned and faced the other people. Polly recognized the manager and his wife, and two middle-aged men, guests of the hotel, who were talking volubly. Lambert, the manager, raised a hand and said, in a surprisingly loud voice:

'Be quiet, gentlemen, if you please.'

They fell silent.

'Parade-ground tactics,' said George, with an inane smile. 'Thank you very much. Mrs. Lambert and gentlemen, I have police authority, and I know you will forgive me for not explaining what happened here. I will gladly discuss it with the police, if you care to send for them—perhaps it will be better if you do. The gentleman who escaped your close attentions was caught in the act of burgling this room, but I don't think he had time to remove anything but the minor valuables.' His voice was like soothing syrup, and in spite of his closed eye and his unimposing appearance, he was quite the strongest personality in the room. 'If Mrs. Lambert will look after Miss Dalton, who has been very brave, I'm sure she would appreciate it. You'll telephone for the police, Mr. Lambert, won't you? And I suppose you haven't a spare beefsteak?'

'Beefsteak!' gasped Lambert.

'Fine cure for black eyes,' said George, cheerfully, 'and is my eye going to be black! Look at it already! Don't you think,' he added, with a sudden change of tone, 'that we ought to leave Mrs. Lambert and Miss Dalton together, gentlemen?'

He ushered the men out of the room and led the way downstairs, talking all the way.

In the small but pleasant hall there stood a large man, more than usually good-looking, although his nose was a trifle too large—or more correctly, was Grecian. This man surveyed the party coming down the stairs, and demanded, in a most cultured voice, whether anyone had sent for a taxi.

'Oh yes,' said George, without batting an eye. 'I want you to take a large parcel to the station for me—it is addressed. You'll find it in my Room—Number 11,' he added, and then raised his hand as if to touch his eye, and in so doing spread out four fingers and a thumb. Toller's room number was 5. 'Will you get it? Thank you so much.' He took two half-crowns out of his pocket, and put them into the large man's hand, saying: 'I can't come up, I've an urgent date with a beefsteak!' He assured Lambert that there was no need to send a maid or a porter up with the taxi-driver, then led the way into Lambert's office, which opened off the front hall. Lambert and the two guests followed.

Not until later did Lambert and the others discover that the 'parcel' was a man whose face was battered very much more than George's, and who needed much support as he walked down the stairs, across the hall, and stepped from the porch to the luxurious limousine standing outside. The limousine had a taxi-meter, but was remarkably modern and smooth running, even for a Bournemouth taxi in the higher category.

Little Lambert, a perky man with a waxed moustache, was satisfied after a police sergeant had called, but Mrs. Lambert was by no means satisfied, because she felt that Miss Dalton, such a *charming* girl, had not been wholly frank. She was disappointed, too—Miss Dalton was not, she thought, the type of young lady whom one would expect to find in a man's bedroom. Hotel-keeping did so disillusion one.

Little Lambert laughed.

'I think there's more in this business than meets the eye, Emily. I'm not really surprised that there has been trouble. I've remembered where we've heard of Toller.'

'I *knew* I'd seen that man before,' said Mrs. Lambert.

'You've seen his photograph,' Lambert told her. 'He's *the* Gabriel Toller.'

'Oh, is he?' murmured Mrs. Lambert, vaguely.

'They say he invented more secret weapons than any man living, during the war,' said Lambert. 'Nearly all electrical devices, I think.'

'What *I* want to know,' said Mrs. Lambert, 'is what Mr. Toller has got to do with Miss Dalton being in that *fool's* room?'

'I think we can take it for granted,' said Lambert, twirling his moustache, 'that George isn't the fool he pretends to be.'

Mrs. Lambert sniffed.

'I don't think Miss Dalton is the girl *she* pretends to be,' she declared. 'The Fool and the girl, they've got to go. Why, you never know what might happen, and if Mr. Larkin saw the girl coming out of his room, or him coming out of her room, the Fool's, I mean, why, he'd probably give notice on the spot, you know how strict he is.'

'He's an old hypocrite,' said Lambert, glumly.

'There's no need to talk like that about a 10-*guinea* guest, winter and summer,' said Mrs. Lambert, 'even if we do reduce his price to 8 guineas in the winter, and it wouldn't surprise me,' continued Mrs. Lambert, heatedly, 'if that girl hasn't got her eyes on *you*.'

'Oh, be sensible,' growled Lambert.

'I am sensible enough,' declared his wife, loftily. 'It is you who lack the common sense to make a real success of this business, Eric. The old gentleman can stay, if he behaves himself, and I'm sure he will, he gave me such a nice smile this morning. You'd better write a note so that they can have it on their breakfast table in the morning, Eric. The Fool and that girl, I mean.'

He knew better than to protest further.

When he went to put the notes by the respective plates, however—it was nearly half-past nine and the dining-room was empty—he found on the Fool's table a well-filled envelope. It was addressed to him. He opened it as he walked back to the office-cum-living-room, and stood reading it while his wife looked up at him, prim faced.

'Eric, what on *earth* are you reading?' she demanded. 'And—Eric! What's that? Where did you get all that money?'

Lambert, who had taken a thick wad of one-pound notes from the envelope, looked over his glasses at his wife and said, in a bewildered voice:

'They've gone.'

'Gone? Who's gone?'

'The Fool, Mr. Toller and Miss Dalton,' said Lambert, sitting down on the arm of a chair. 'George has written a silly note, he says that all three of them think the air of the West Cliff is better than on the East Cliff. He's enclosed two weeks' money for each of them, in lieu of notice, and says their cases are packed and will be collected at ten o'clock.'

4

ALL SHAPES AND SIZES

P ink, plump and delicious,' murmured George Henry
George, in a soft voice. 'Isn't she?'

'Oh, a pretty piece, I grant you,' said his companion.

The companion was the taxi-driver of the previous day.
They were sitting together at the edge of a grass court,
watching Polly Dalton playing a spirited game with another
large man, who was remarkably like George's companion.
Many people, seeing the two together, thought they were
twins; in fact, they were cousins, and their surname was
Errol.

Mark Errol was playing, Mike sitting in a deck-chair with
George Henry George on the grass by his side.

The tennis court was at the back of a large, modern house.
Until a month before it had been in the market, a hotel 'furnished throughout and with every modern convenience'. It
had been bought by a man unknown locally, and from the first
day 'No Vacancies' had appeared on the gate, the front door and
one window.

The people who lived on either side saw that it was full,

mostly with male guests, and assumed that the new owner had brought with him a good connection.

'She has what it takes, too,' declared George. 'I mean, no vapours about Plump Polly, she backed me up like a good 'un, and although we haven't told her anything yet, she's pretty patient about it. Not many women would be. I wonder when Loftus or Big Chief Craigie will get here. We mustn't go into details until one of 'em comes, I suppose?'

'We must not,' said Mike. 'That's most strictly forbidden. One of them will turn up today, though I shouldn't work yourself up about that.'

'How long have you worked for them?' asked George.

'Six or seven years,' said Mike, absently.

'And they've kept you busy all that time?'

'Pretty busy, on the whole,' said Mike. He smiled lazily at his companion.

'How long have you been one of the crowd?'

'Six months,' said George. 'I was transferred from M.I.9, of course. I was three years in that shop, and heard a bit about Craigie, Loftus and the Department, but I didn't really believe it.'

'Departmental jealousy,' said Mike.

'Oh, I wouldn't say that. The stories were a bit tall, you know. About this and that. *Is* Craigie a close personal friend of Herbert Mattley?'

'He's well in with the Prime Minister,' said Errol, 'in a manner of speaking. Craigie doesn't make many mistakes, you know, and he has a nose for the right thing to do. You probably don't know Craigie well enough to like him yet,' went on Mike, 'but you will when you've been with us a little longer. He seems a bit cold and dry at first.'

Department Z, of which they had talked, was a small and little-known section of the Intelligence Service. Among the other branches its work was legendary—and, in some degree, discredited. Its tally of agents in England was rarely more than twenty, although it could call on the police and other branches of intelligence when the need arose. But there were agents of the Department in most of the world's capitals and in many smaller cities, and many strange matters passed through its hands. Or, more accurately, the hands of Gordon Craigie and Bill Loftus, who worked in the office, Loftus as Craigie's assistant.

Loftus had lost a leg in the Department's service.

In England, the work was highly specialized—counterespionage of a particular kind, against highly organized spy rings. Now and again those spy rings became not only active but violent—and where there was violence of that kind, there was also Department Z.

All these things George Henry George, the newest recruit, knew quite well.

The couple on the court finished their set, gravely shook hands, and strolled towards the house. George jumped up and had iced drinks waiting for them, for the day was hot, and the heat on the court would have been overpowering but for the ring of tall pine trees which surrounded the back garden of the hotel, which was called *The Pines*. A few spectral clouds floated lazily across the sky, at a great height, and the shrubs and flowers which abounded were besieged by butterflies and bees. A few wasps hummed about the lemonade and lager as Polly and Mark Errol drew up. Mark was perspiring a little, but Polly looked as fresh as when she had started; her plumpness was deceiving.

'Here we are, tuppence a glass, fresh from the lemongroves of Sicily and the premises of the famous Pilsener,' said George, brightly. 'Lager, Polly?'

'No, thanks,' she said, 'lemonade.'

'You won't get drunk on Pilsener,' George said.

'I won't get drunk on anything,' said Polly, 'I never touch alcohol.'

The remark produced an effect far greater than she expected. The Errols stared at her incredulously, and George again went pink. Beer was part of the staple diet of Department men. Seeing this concern, Polly smiled serenely, and said that she had not the slightest objection to others drinking lager or whatever they chose, provided they did not try to force it on her.

'There is one thing which I do mind,' declared Polly, accepting a cigarette and a glass of iced lemonade, 'and that is the mystery with which you all surround yourselves. I'm tired of being told that I will learn all about it later, it just isn't good enough. This isn't a normal hotel, is it?'

'Well, hardly,' said Mike. 'It's a—'

'Hostel for respectable young men,' Mark finished for him.

'Respectable?' queried Polly, with a sniff. 'I'm not at all sure that I ought to stay here. There isn't another woman in the place, so far as I've been able to see.'

'Strange women, our women,' said Mike Errol.

'Silent,' said Mark.

'If that's a hint that I'm not to ask questions, it isn't any good,' said Polly, spiritedly. 'There are nine men in all including the Professor—and all of you know one another, except the Professor. Don't you?' she demanded.

'We're acquainted,' admitted Mike.

He leaned forward and smiled, but he was serious. 'Before the day's out you'll know what this is all about, Polly, and you won't regret having been so patient. Don't present an ultimatum just yet.'

Polly looked at him thoughtfully and promised that she would wait until dinner-time.

It was then a little after three o'clock, almost twenty-four hours from the moment when she had heard the scratching at the door next to her room. On all that had happened, she was vague. She had had grave doubts, at first, as to the wisdom of leaving the *Mayberry* and coming to the hotel which George recommended, but George had a way with him, and he had assured her that the terms would be no higher than those of *Mayberry*. The food was more like that of a luxury hotel, however, the appointments were remarkably good, and she was a little uneasy about that. Eight guineas a week was her limit for the three weeks' holiday in front of her.

During tea, young men appeared as if from nowhere. Most of them were large and all of them were flippant. There was a round-faced, curly-haired young man named Dunster, Teddy Dunster, who was obviously taken by her, and a dark, sallow youth with pomaded hair, named Grey—Guy Grey—who watched her with languid, but interested eyes. The names of the others escaped her. They were a boisterous crowd, all shapes and sizes, and they reminded her of a touring cricket eleven which had once stayed for several nights at an hotel where she had been staying with her mother.

After tea she went to her room to change. Various young men passed her and beamed. She changed into a frock of apple-green linen and put on light brown sandals, and then applied herself to the increasingly difficult task of writing home.

At half-past five, while she was still writing, there was a tap at the door. She said, 'Come in,' and looked round.

A tall, fair-haired, smiling woman entered.

'Why, hallo,' said Polly, surprised and pleased.

'I thought I would let you know that you're no longer the only woman in the party,' said the newcomer. They shook hands. 'I'm Christine Loftus, you'll meet my husband soon.'

'Is he like the rest of these...' Polly hesitated, and then added, with a laugh, 'nitwits?'

'Sometimes,' laughed Christine. 'They're much the same.'

She wore a flowered frock of great simplicity, and had a grace of carriage which Polly needlessly envied. There was in her something of the quality which was in all the men—a quality to which Polly could not put a name, but which was nevertheless, apparent. Christine's eyes were grey and laughing, and she was more than ordinarily good-looking. Her hair was curly, short, and attractive.

'Do sit down,' said Polly. 'I *am* glad you've arrived. I felt a little bit *de trop.*'

'I expect you did,' said Christine, sitting in a small armchair by the window. 'You needn't. I was adjured by Mike and Mark Errol, George and several others to promise you the story—*the* story—between now and dinner-time. And I've come in advance,' she added, 'to tell you that you need not stay here unless you really want to—after you've heard what there is to hear, of course. They'll probably ask you to do something for them, and there is absolutely no compulsion.'

'I suppose not,' said Polly, doubtfully.

Christine laughed.

'I suppose I'm making it more mysterious. I mustn't talk so much.' She leaned forward and looked out of the window, and then she asked: 'Had you ever met Professor Toller before?'

'No,' said Polly. 'I didn't even know his name until George made some silly remark about him having been attacked nine times. At least, I thought it was a silly remark at the time, but now I'm not so sure.'

'George wanted to try to find out whether you knew anything about him,' said Christine, and went on quickly: 'He now swears that you didn't, but—'

She was interrupted by another tap at the door, followed by a deep voice:

'You there, Christine?'

'Yes, darling.' Christine stood up.

'We're ready when you are,' said the man.

'We're ready now,' said Christine.

'Do come in,' called Polly.

The door opened and a huge man entered. He was much taller even than Christine, six feet three or four, and his shoulders were vast. He had a large, rather plain face—a homey face—and he was smiling. Without the smile he would have looked wooden, rather like the man who had attacked her and escaped the day before. Polly wished she had not seen a like-ness; it worried her.

'This is my husband,' Christine said. 'Bill, I've promised Miss Dalton that you'll tell her everything you can.'

'So I should think,' said Loftus, in a firm voice. He extended a large hand; she expected to find it flabby, but it was as hard as leather. When he went out of the room ahead of them, she saw that he limped, but it was not until later that she learned that his right leg was an artificial one. He towered above them as he led the way downstairs, and then into a room marked *'Private'.*

George and the Errols were there, and Professor Gabriel Toller, whom she had seen only once before while at *The Pines*. There were two others. One was a compact, sturdily-built man who looked older than any of the others except Toller. He was dressed in brown, his thick, wavy hair was brown, and his eyes were hazel. When he was introduced, he bowed gravely. He was good-looking, with a close-clipped brown moustache that spread over the whole of his upper lip. The second stranger was a short, almost hunchbacked middle-aged Jew, whose presence surprised her. He had a Punch-like face, long, curved nose and long, curved chin almost meeting, and he looked sad—as if some deep sorrow weighed upon him. One side of his face was badly scarred.

The brown man was introduced as Bruce Hammond, the Jew as Hoffmann.

Loftus lowered himself into an armchair, which was only just large enough for him. He stretched his legs out straight in front of him, and, after much deliberation, began:

'Miss Dalton, I'm going to be brief, I'm probably going to be puzzling, and I'm going to open with a question. Have you ever met Professor Toller before?'

'Only yesterday,' said Polly, 'and I've already answered that question several times.'

'Sorry,' said Loftus, and looked at the bearded man. 'Professor, what about you?'

'No, I had not seen Miss Dalton until yesterday at breakfast,' said the Professor.

'Thank you.' Loftus took a deep drink of beer, replacing his tankard with a sigh, and went on as if he had not paused. 'Professor Toller, Miss Dalton, is a scientist of eminence, who has made many discoveries of great importance to the country—and to the United Nations—and who is now working on another of equal importance. Once he worked for Dakers, a prominent armament firm, but now he is employed by the Government. You will not expect me to tell you what it is. By unexpected chance you were given a room at the *Mayberry* next to the Professor's. We were taking care of him, and we knew that the room had been booked by a couple named Merryweather, and we suspected that Merryweather wanted the room so that he could gain access to the Professor's. The Merryweathers didn't turn up until you were safely installed in the room, and then only the man arrived. That gave rise to some misunderstanding—George, rightly, thought you might be there on behalf of the said Merry-weathers.'

'I've never heard of the Merryweathers,' declared Polly.

'We now know that the Lamberts gave you the room without telling you of the change until you were there,' said Loftus, with a twinkle in his eye, 'so George's suspicions are proved groundless. Now you have the bones of the story, Miss Dalton. The Professor was in danger, we wanted to know from whom, we took considerable precautions to save him from injury. George took from his bed, yesterday, a little gadget which had been put there by the man you saw trying to break into the room. It was a time-bomb, more latterly known as a mine.' Loftus spoke mildly.

Polly stared. 'An *explosive*!'

'Bombs do bang,' said Loftus, apologetically. 'It would have blown him up, bed and all. So, you see, the idea that there was villainy afoot was not far wrong,' said Loftus. 'You are entitled to know that, equally entitled to know that everyone in this room, except yourself and my wife, who came down to keep you company, knew of what was planned and was working to prevent it.'

'All of you?' asked Polly, in a bewildered voice.

'In one way or another, all of us,' said Loftus. 'We have different jobs to do, of course. The chief one just now is to find out who wants to kill the Professor.'

'I suppose so,' said Polly, and looked at the old man, whose eyes were twinkling at her. She said, with warmth: 'I think he takes it marvellously!'

'I am quite used to danger,' murmured the Professor.

'So are we all,' said Loftus, lightly. 'Well, now. George showed you his card. We all have similar cards. We would not have told you more but for two things. One is that although one man who broke into the *Mayberry* was caught, and proved to be Merryweather, the other escaped. He has friends. He knows that you helped George. While you stay in Bournemouth, you may be approached and questioned. In fact, it's almost certain that you will be.'

He paused, and Polly said: 'Well, I needn't answer him.'

'Of course not,' said Loftus, looking taken aback and embarrassed. 'That is, if he—or they—don't exert too much pressure. You had one experience of their methods yesterday, didn't you?'

Polly fingered her throat. It was still a little tender, and there were bruises beneath her ears; she recalled the pain as the hard-faced man had gripped her, and she realized suddenly what Loftus meant. She coloured, and did not speak.

'Now our problem is a ticklish one,' said Loftus. 'Merryweather, it proves, has very little knowledge of the other people involved with him, and we must find them. Operative word, must. They will try to prevent us, and they will probably use violence. They know most of us by sight and they are not likely to strike at any one of us. They may try again at the Professor, but that's by no means certain. If *you* were to stay in Bournemouth, however—'

'Do you want me to *help*?' exclaimed Polly, aghast.

'We would like you to help,' said Loftus, 'but we know that you may think it's too risky. It *will* be risky. If you go away, of course, we shall meet any expense to which you're put.'

Polly, sitting near the middle of the room, felt every eye turned towards her. George was just behind her, with the Errols, and their gaze seemed to be burning into her neck. Even Toller was staring, and the sad eyes of the little Jew seemed full of appeal.

Appeal! They were all asking her to stay in Bournemouth and to take this risk!

She spoke after a long pause. Her voice was remarkably steady:

'It would help if I know who you are. I can't even be sure that you've any authority at all.'

'We can satisfy you about that,' said Loftus. 'We are—well, call us Special Branch men.'

'I wish you could tell me more,' said Polly, slowly.

'We haven't treated you too badly,' said Loftus, 'and we can't go further. There's no need to make a snap decision— think about it. You can have until breakfast tomorrow. If you can say one way or the other after dinner tonight, it will be helpful. Remember, no compulsion,' he added with a quick smile. 'There is one other thing, before we go. I've painted the picture fairly black. It might be only a dull shade of grey. These people are not fools. They will have found out as much about you as we have by now—'

'What do you mean?' demanded Polly, sharply.

Loftus laughed. 'Name, age, place of birth, place of business, home address, record and reputation! No, no awkward questions have been asked anywhere, but as soon as your name was mentioned we had to find out what we could. This man will have done the same. You've been here, and presumably you have learned something—that is how his mind will probably work. He may try to bribe you to tell him what you've learned. If you're going to join us, we'll prime you with a story to tell him. At no time will we leave you with him for long, and we shall always know where you are. You will be most closely watched. At best, it will be a chance encounter with him or one of his envoys, a talk over lunch or dinner or tea—perhaps at an hotel, more likely at a private house. After they've had one interview with you, I don't think there'll be much to worry about.'

Polly said, slowly:

'I have always wanted to spend a holiday in Bournemouth.'

'Don't be too hasty,' said Christine, unexpectedly.

Polly turned to her. 'Will you be here all the time?'

'Yes,' said Christine, 'if you stay.'

'I will,' said Polly.

There was a moment of silence among those men of all shapes and sizes. Then Loftus smiled, leaned forward, and patted her shoulder. Mark and Mike shared an approving sentence between them, and George squeezed her forearm until it hurt. Hammond, who had sat there, a brown man as if in a brown study, looked up with an unexpectedly attractive smile, and the Professor said, 'Thank you, my dear, thank you very much indeed,' in his deep voice.

Yet it was Hoffmann who impressed her most.

The shadows were lifted from his eyes. It was only for a moment, while he looked at her, and he made no move and did not speak, but the smile on that scarred face, the sudden lightness in the sad eyes, did more than anything else to convince her that she had made the right decision.

As she turned to leave the room with George, she spoke in an aside:

'Probably nothing will come of it.'

'Bless your heart, nothing that will harm you!' said George, with feeling. 'Our enemies will use the velvet glove, and you'll probably be given the finest dinner Bournemouth can provide while you deliver up these specially prepared secrets.'

She looked at him severely, and said:

'You already owe me the finest dinner in England.'

'Good Lord!' exclaimed George. 'So I do!'

At seven o'clock, not quite sure whether she wanted a *tête-à-tête* with George, dressed in a cocktail dress of royal blue, Polly left *The Pines* on foot, with George at her side. He was a changed George, resplendent in a dinner-jacket suit, but no less light-hearted. She expected some of the others to follow them, but she saw no one whom she knew, and after five minutes, as they walked along the roads of West Cliff towards the Square, she was laughing helplessly at her companion's drollery. Yet she was not so absorbed in him as to fail to see a man who moved suddenly into a doorway. She caught only a glimpse of him, but his was a face she was never likely to forget.

She gripped George's arm.

'George—that man!'

'Man?' said George, vaguely.

'The man who was in your room.'

'Oh,' said George. 'Him. Or should it be he? Don't look round!' he added, softly. He tightened his grip on her arm and made her walk past the doorway, although she found it hard to keep her eyes averted.

'Why didn't you *do* something?' demanded Polly.

'My dear lass, what? A little chap like me and a big chap like him? Phoo! I'm not a hero. And if you'll laugh gaily, as you were born to, you'll see his reflection in the window of the corner shop,' he added, without a change of tone. 'If he's following us, that's fine.'

She watched the shop window closely, and caught another glimpse of the hard-faced man.

5

MR. RUTTER AND OTHERS

Y ou *must* do something,' urged Polly.

'I am. I'm taking the pinkest, plum—pluckiest girl in Bournemouth out to dinner,' said George.

'I *won't* stand this fooling,' said Polly, half-angry, half-serious. 'There's the very man you want, you needn't pretend you're afraid of him. I know better than that.'

'Such praise!' said George. 'Be a pet, and don't worry about him. He is doing what we expected, keeping an eye on you. Er—you don't think he got away yesterday because he'd set his mind on it, do you?'

'*What?*' gasped Polly.

'We walked instead of getting a cab, because we hoped he would follow. In turn, he is being followed.'

'I haven't seen anyone else I know.'

'I should think not! Why do you think a grateful country pays us a pittance if we don't know our job? He's been followed, all the same. Now shake yourself out of it, Polly, don't worry. Nothing will happen tonight—er—that is, nothing that matters. I shall make the most outrageous love to you while we're at the *Norfolk*—nothing barred except being thrown out. Mind?'

'What *are*—' began Polly, and intended to add: 'you talking about.' She stopped, however, and looked at him with a thoughtful expression. After a pause, while he led her across the Square, a meeting-place of many thoroughfares ringed about by tall buildings and fine gardens, and that evening packed with people, she said: 'Do you mean to say that even this dinner is a duty?'

'Duty? Benighted word! Never a greater delight,' said George, 'but if we can help to pull the wool over the eyes of the man with the Iron Face, why not? Don't take all I say too seriously, and bear with me as patiently as you can.'

She noticed him glance over her shoulder, a quick, almost furtive glance, and then his foolish grin returned. 'You're not as quick on the uptake as usual, perhaps it's a case of wilful blindness. I am going to pretend to have fallen for you, figure, face and blinkers. Old Iron Face will scent romance. He would like to feel that you could twist one of the boys about your little finger.'

'I see,' said Polly. 'What must I do? Return your soulful gaze?'

'How nice of you not to say cow-like,' said George. 'As you wish. No rebuffs that are too obvious—boredom with a buffoon, if you like, but not too much boredom. As a girl might react to an ass with oodles of money.'

'I see,' said Polly, with studied calm.

'Did I tell you,' he added, as they went into the lounge, a quiet and luxurious place, 'that you are looking very lovely tonight.'

'Need you start now?' demanded Polly.

'Not all I say will be dishonest,' declared George. 'Shall we go straight in, or will you have a drink here or at the bar?'

'I'd like a tomato juice cocktail,' said Polly. 'I don't mind where.'

'Oh yes, of course,' said George, wilting a trifle. 'Tail, cock, juice, tomato, one. Damn it, two!' he added, explosively. 'Waiter!'

She admitted, when they reached *The Pines*, a little after ten o'clock, that it had been one of the liveliest and entertaining evenings imaginable, and George was not displeased. When he had delivered her to Christine, who was with several of the various shapes and sizes in the large lounge, he went to the door marked *'Private'*, and tapped a light tattoo. Loftus bade him enter. Loftus and Hammond were there alone, and both looked up with a quick smile.

'Fair dos,' said George. 'Any luck with Iron Face?'

'We trailed him home,' said Loftus. 'His place is now closely watched, and it's a good start. What do you make of Polly now?'

'She'll see it through,' said George. 'She's much tougher than she looks. She's still a bit puzzled, and a little disgruntled because we haven't told her more, but she's interested. She has the kind of quick mind which is made for the job. Don't worry about plump, pink Polly! She has,' he added, after a reflective pause, during which they grinned at him, 'a distinct portion of personality plus.'

'Plus George Henry,' said Loftus, sardonically. 'Have a look at this.'

'This' was a sheet of quarto paper, typewritten in single spacing. George's expression grew owlish, and he read it through quickly once, then more slowly. He looked up with an absent-minded smile, then read it for a third time.

'That's fine,' he said. 'It sticks near enough to the truth to make it plausible. The only alteration I'd suggest,' he added, 'is

—type it in double-spacing before she reads it. It'll be easier to learn, I think.'

'There's something in that,' admitted Loftus.

'Thanks,' said George. 'So we've the story that Polly is to tell the bad man. I hope Iron Face doesn't interview her in person,' he went on, slowly. 'She doesn't like him one little bit, and I don't want her to have unnecessary unpleasantness from the gentleman.'

He did not sound hopeful.

Polly received the typewritten document from Christine after she had gone to bed. The story which she was to tell, if she were questioned by Iron Face or anyone else, was comprehensive and straightforward. Some of it she knew, some—the 'information' she was to pass on—was quite new to her.

'I'll have it off by heart tomorrow morning,' she promised.

In spite of being excited, for her mind was humming with questions, theories and ideas, she went to sleep before midnight, and did not wake up until a maid brought her morning tea. It was half-past eight, and the sun was shining over the bay, which she could see from the window opposite the bed. The view was glorious.

On the previous evening the man whom George called Iron Face, and who was known to his acquaintances as Rutter, did not himself follow George and Polly to the *Norfolk*. Another man, short, slim and dark, did that for him. Soon afterwards the little man was joined by a tiny woman who was too flamboyant to be true to life. He took her into the dining-room at the *Norfolk*, and afterwards they followed George and Polly to *The Pines*. The house was already being watched by another of the men who worked for Rutter, and the little man hurried back to Rutter's house.

That, in turn, was being watched by men of Department Z.

A man opened the door, and the little fellow went in, tapped at a door on the left of the small hall, and was told to enter.

Rutter was alone.

He had a red swelling beneath one eye, a result of his encounter with George, but otherwise looked unscathed.

He offered Lodge a cigarette, and the little man took one and sat on the edge of his chair.

'Well?' asked Rutter.

'I don't think there's much doubt about them, Mr. Rutter,' said Lodge, whose thin, spotted face held a hopeful look. 'I certainly don't think there's much doubt *there*. The man's crazy about her.'

'In twenty-four hours?' asked Rutter, sceptically.

'Well, that's what I think,' said Lodge, defensively. 'And she's not struck on him, that's as clear as the nose on your face, Mr. Rutter. If you ask me, she sees money in him—and he's got plenty, you can tell that.'

When Lodge had gone, Rutter reached for the telephone, which was on the small table with the lamp. He gave a London number, waited for a few minutes, and was answered at last by a man whose voice sounded young and pleasant.

'Maurice speaking,' said the man.

'What have you found out about the Dalton girl?' asked Rutter. No one standing a yard away could have heard the words.

'Oh, hallo, Boss!' said Maurice, lightly. 'I've got the story, for what it's worth. No sign of a connection with the Z men.

Lives with her widowed mother in a flat at Putney. Not well off—she earns the living, eight hundred pounds a year for a small firm of accountants. She's clever at figures. Aged twenty-five.'

'What else?' asked Rutter.

'She's what everyone calls a "nice" girl,' said Maurice, with a faint sneer. 'Teetotaller—Low Church—has worked in the same place for nine years. Father was killed in the last war, after losing a fortune. They came down in the world. Holiday once a year—mother and daughter usually spend it together, but this year an uncle arrived a few days before, and fell ill. He's at the flat. The mother's nursing him.'

'Is the uncle vouched for?' demanded Rutter.

'Visits them regularly,' said Maurice. 'She isn't connected with the Z men, old boy.'

Rutter's lips curved in distaste at the familiarity, but he uttered no reproof. After a long pause, he said:

'All right. Come down early tomorrow morning. I want you to get to know her.'

He rang off without saying good-bye.

At half-past one, Rutter stirred and looked at his watch.

Then he heard a car.

It turned into the street, which was on the East Cliff, and the high-powered whine was clearly audible. Rutter grew more tense. The car pulled up, there was a creaking sound followed by the slamming of a door. Rutter remained impassive, and did not get up when the front-door bell rang. Someone moved in the house, footsteps pattered down the stairs, and then the front door opened.

'Good evening, sir,' said a woman.

'Good evening,' said a man.

For the first time Rutter's lips curved in a smile—a barely perceptible one, noticeably only because his face was usually so set. He stood up. The woman outside tapped at the door and when he called 'come in' she opened it and stood aside. A man stepped into the room, tall, arresting-looking.

'All right, Maude,' said Rutter. 'You may go to bed.'

'Thank you, sir.' The woman, old, wizened and bent, nodded and withdrew, closing the door. The visitor did not move, but smiled at Rutter, who backed a pace, as if admiring clothes on a model. He moved round the newcomer, the smile showing several times again. Not once did his visitor move, until the inspection was finished. Then he stepped towards a chair and said:

'Well, Mr. Rutter, will I do?'

'It couldn't be better,' said Rutter. 'I didn't believe it was possible!'

'I thought you'd be pleased,' said the other, and his voice was different. Before it had been deep and resonant—practically the same as Professor Gabriel Toller's. Now it was higher, and he laughed complacently. 'I'm an artist at this business, Mr. Rutter, and the beard and hair were a godsend—nothing is easier to copy.'

He sat down—a man who looked in every particular like Gabriel Toller. He even rested his hands upon his knees, imitating Toller's mannerism.

6
ENTER MAURICE

All those people who worked for Rutter, and there were many in various capacities, agreed on two points. He was not easily satisfied, and he was personally prepared to take great pains to get exactly what he wanted. It was not surprising, therefore, that after the first excess of enthusiasm, which had brought the reluctant smile to his lips, he switched on the ceiling light, told the imposing visitor to sit where it shone fully on him, and then took a dozen photographs from a bookshelf. They were likenesses of the real Gabriel Toller, taken from different angles. Rutter took one at a time, and, holding it in his hand, made another complete circuit of the visitor and the chair.

It was a long process, and the visitor spoke in the middle of it.

'I don't mind this one bit, Mr. Rutter, in fact I think you're very wise to check up, but I've had a long journey, you know, and I'm famished.'

'Oh yes,' said Rutter. 'I'd forgotten. Wait.' He went out.

The visitor did not move his position while Rutter was out

of the room. The hard-faced man returned, carrying a tray, and the double of Gabriel Toller rubbed his hands in anticipation. There were several kinds of sandwiches and a generous portion of veal and ham pie, together with whisky-and-soda.

'Well, I must say that's a cheerful sight, I really must,' said the visitor. 'May I break off for ten minutes?'

'Yes,' said Rutter. 'What kind of journey did you have?'

'*Very* comfortable,' said the other, with a broad smile which showed that his teeth, like Gabriel Toller's, were small, white and even—good dentures which would deceive some people at a casual glance. 'You can trust me for that.'

'I wasn't thinking of your comfort, Kelly,' said Rutter.

'No, of course not,' said Kelly. 'I see what you mean, Mr. Rutter. I took the greatest precautions. You can rely on me. I started from Birmingham in daylight, of course, but I took the utmost precautions not to be seen. I stepped straight from the door into the car, with a handkerchief at my face, and once in the car, I drew the curtains. It was quite impossible for anyone to see me.'

'Go on,' said Rutter.

Kelly swallowed a large piece of pie. The conversation was spoiling his enjoyment of the meal, and his eyes—grey, like Toller's—took on an expression which was never seen in those of the Professor. He was scared of Mr. Rutter.

'I gave Peel the most careful instructions. He stopped by the side of the road for several minutes every half-hour, and at no time were we passed by the *same* car. There was no indication that we were followed, no indication at all. You need not worry about that, Mr. Rutter.'

Rutter grunted, but made no intelligible comment.

When he had finished his inspection, he gave Kelly permission to take the tray upstairs with him. Then he also went up, not to his own room but to an attic where three men were sleeping. One of them was a small, bald-headed man. Little patches of hair over his temples were, surprisingly, jet black. Rutter shook him roughly. The man was awake on the instant, and sat up like a mechanical doll. The other men stirred but seemed not to wake.

'Yes, Mr. Rutter.' The words came like clockwork.

'What kind of a journey did you have, Peel?' asked Rutter.

'Oh, very good,' said Peel. 'No trouble. I didn't miss nothing. There was an Austin 10 I didn't like the look of. It turned off at Oxford, though, I never saw it again.'

'All right,' said Rutter.

He turned away from Peel, and looked dispassionately at the others. One man was too large for the small bed, and he slept with his mouth open. He had red hair and red stubble. The other was a small, oily-looking individual who had his knees bent.

'If you two are awake, open your eyes,' said Rutter.

Two pairs of eyes opened instantly.

Rutter nodded, and went out. In the passage, he was smiling again. He was training some of his staff to work in the way he wanted them to. That particular couple would never allow anyone to enter their room without waking them, and yet they could feign sleep excellently. That was the advantage of employing ex-soldiers—all men with bad reputations, who, for some reason or other, had been dismissed from Service. Ex-soldiers had discipline, and they obeyed automatically. Rutter maintained that discipline at least as thoroughly as a sergeant-major, and considered his men to be always on duty.

The clock near by struck three when he reached the hall.

The only sign that he felt tired was a narrowing of his eyes, which were slightly red at the rims. He went straight to the telephone, and tapped his fingers impatiently because it was not immediately answered. It was a private line, secretly and illegally installed.

A man answered at last—the voice of a man named Hemmingway Noel.

Noel's was an unusual voice, deep, pleasant and mellow, and for the first time that evening a man addressed Rutter without a polite or obsequious 'Mr.' Rutter seemed to expect this, and although there was no difference in the tone of his voice, he spoke as if to a man whom he respected.

'Kelly is here, and is perfect,' he said.

'Good!' said Noel, heartily.

'He was not followed from Birmingham,' said Rutter. 'I doubt whether anyone knew he was there, and I'm quite sure no one knew what he was doing.'

'I should hope not,' said Noel.

'I learned from a newspaperman that Merryweather has not talked,' said Rutter, 'and I think we can rely on him. In any case he knows neither of us, so there is no great danger.'

'Go on,' said Noel.

'I am having Maurice down, to try to interest the Dalton girl,' said Rutter. 'I don't think we can move until the day after tomorrow, but that should be soon enough. We may have to wait until Friday. Much depends on the pull which Maurice can get over the girl.'

'Tell him to be very careful,' said Noel.

Rutter said: 'I'll promise him an extra hundred pounds if he succeeds, that will make Maurice exert himself.'

Noel gave a soft, amused laugh.

'You know your men, Rutter, don't you? That's as well. As for time—I shall be most disappointed if we do not have Toller with us in the flesh by Monday. That gives you nearly a week.'

* * *

Polly Dalton first noticed the tall, remarkably handsome man at lunchtime the next day. He was sitting alone in the popular café above a big store near the Square, and he looked at her frequently. So did other men, but none of them was alone and none was quite so handsome. True, this man's looks were not of the kind to appeal to her. He must be middle-aged, but was dressed like a youth. He had fine eyes, and with them he ogled even the waitress, whom most people would have thought past the age of flirtation. He was, thought Polly, a man who could not resist making an impression on a woman—any woman.

She felt inwardly excited, although she was outwardly calm. Odd, foolish remarks which George had made the previous evening kept passing through her mind. She tried to stop them by repeating the instructions which she had received later, but she did not meet with complete success.

In a corner, with two men whom she did not recognize, were Mike and Mark Errol. They had not paid her any attention; nor did they seem interested in the man who caught her eye.

When she got up and went to pay her bill, the handsome man did the same thing. At the pay-desk he knocked against her, and was immediately excessive in his apologies. His voice was tenor, attractive enough—in fact, just a little too attractive. At a guess she would have dubbed him an actor. She wondered who was appearing at the Pavilion that week; she had meant to look several times, but it had slipped her memory.

'I really am terribly sorry,' he said. 'I do hope that I did not hurt you.'

'Not at all,' murmured Polly, for the third time.

'You are more than kind,' he said. 'Isn't it a positively *glorious* day?'

'Yes,' said Polly, perfunctorily, but her heart was beating fast; it seemed too much to think that this encounter was purely chance. Was this the emissary from Iron Face, or was he a man looking for a companion for the day, the night, or the next few weeks? She had few illusions.

She had put her bill down on the glass plate, preparatory to taking out her money. So had he. The cashier said, 'Thank you, sir,' and pushed both bills, with a part torn off, back to the man.

'No, please!' said Polly, at once.

'I do hope you will allow me to make up for my clumsiness in that way,' said Maurice, with his most flourishing smile. 'I deserve to pay for it, I assure you.'

'I don't think—' began Polly.

'Please,' he urged. He bent his head a little and spoke close to her ear. Then he cupped her elbow in his hand, and added before she could object: 'Look, the lift is just going down.' He signalled to the attendant, who waited for them. The lift was already nearly full, and they were pressed together; he kept his hand on her elbow, and she discovered that he smelt faintly of perfume.

'Do you know Bournemouth well?' he asked.

'Not very well,' said Polly.

'It is a town of great charm,' said Maurice, portentiously. 'It reminds me vividly of a Riviera resort, with its gaiety, its carefree atmosphere, its modern buildings and the really *superb* gardens. Do you know the Riviera?'

'I wouldn't compare Bournemouth with Nice,' said Polly.

The lift jolted a little as they went down to the ground floor, and he was unable to go on talking.

She slipped away as soon as they came to a standstill, for she did not want to throw herself at him, although she was tingling with excitement, now fully convinced that this was the man of whom she had been warned.

She was looking at some dresses in a showcase, not without envy, when she saw his shadow close to her. He paused, and said softly: 'May I have the real pleasure—the privilege—of showing you what is, I believe, the most beautiful spot in Bournemouth?'

'Really,' said Polly. She hoped that she was not acting her part too gawkishly. The truth was that she found it difficult to say anything to the creature.

'Oh, I am quite serious,' Maurice assured her. 'It is a spot which few people visit—comparatively few—because it is a little distance from the centre of the town. The crowds—how I abominate them!'

'People *do* flock together,' Polly said.

'Exactly! As sheep! Masses of humanity, teeming crowds, hot, smelly—*noisome*!' They were walking along the street, and before she realized what he was doing, be beckoned a taxi. 'Branksome Chine,' he said to the driver, and in a moment she was sitting with him in the back of the car, a little taken aback. Maurice was, after all, a determined man.

The taxi drew up near the beach at Branksome Chine.

'Wait, driver,' said Maurice.

Cupping her elbow again, he led Polly to the beach, and then pointed towards the bay. The cliffs were topped by many houses and one huge white building that caught the sun and, although square and solid, fitted harmoniously into the loveliness of the skyline. In the distance, white and glistening, were the cliffs of the Isle of Wight, and a little way from them, the Needles. The sandy cliff, topped with palm trees where there were no houses, the light gold of the sand and the clear blue water with its fringe of white foam, fascinated her. A few small craft moved slowly in the bay.

'There is no finer view,' said Maurice, in a hushed voice.

He might be right about that, thought Polly, but he was wrong about the people; there were still crowds. He seemed oblivious of them, and continued to talk in that earnest, attractive voice.

She was not properly conscious of the way the afternoon passed. His voice had a soothing quality, and made her feel tired and yet rested at the same time. She no longer heartily disliked him, although not once had his eyes shone with the sparkle of humour which made George Henry George's glow. Somehow, however, he seemed to take control of her.

He asked no questions, but went on with his interminable talk of beauty.

She had tea with him at a small café.

She went to the Pavilion with him, and there he booked seats for that night's theatre performance.

She had dinner with him, without going to *The Pines* to change.

She sat through the play, which he criticized in whispers, to her annoyance because she was absorbed—and to the greater annoyance of the people near by.

'And now,' he said, when they were outside, 'I must see you home. My dear young lady, I have *never* enjoyed such a day— never! It has proved what I have always believed—kindred spirits need nothing but their own company. I have not even asked your name. You have not asked mine! We have talked intellectually, of the wonder of beauty and the higher forms of art, and although your knowledge is haphazard—forgive me, but it is,' he squeezed her arm gently—'it has been an experience to see the impression which it has made on your fresh, virginal mind. I hope I may have the delight of your company for at least a *part* of tomorrow.'

'Well—' began Polly.

'Where I leave you tonight, I will find you tomorrow, with the fresh dew of morning on your brow and the light of the early sun reflected in your eyes,' intoned Maurice. 'Where are you staying?'

'At *The Pines*,' said Polly, faintly.

'Ah, *The Pines*,' breathed Maurice.

In the half-light from a sky still lit by the afterglow of the brilliant day, he succeeded in finding a taxi. Many cars were drawn up at the kerb, and a milling crowd of people streamed towards Westover Road; the busy scene was softened by the subdued, coloured light. He opened the door of the taxi—and then for the first time he did something she did not expect, as if he were jerked out of his mood of brooding, almost melancholy calm. His hand was on her elbow, and she felt his grip tighten. For the first time since morning she experienced a twinge of fear.

He said, in an urgent whisper:

'Tomorrow, here, eleven o'clock. Driver—' his voice rose. '*The Pines Hotel.*' He put money into the taxi-driver's hand, but he was looking past the taxi, and Polly saw the man at whom he was looking.

Hoffmann was standing near the playing fountain, lit by many coloured lights, outside the Pavilion. He was not looking at Maurice, but his presence had obviously given Maurice a shock. As soon as the door was closed, Maurice looked at her, smiled absently, and disappeared. The sad eyes of the little Jew followed him—and then suddenly were turned towards Polly with a quick, transforming smile.

7

'TOMORROW, HERE'

Nice fellow?' asked George, brightly.

'Charming,' said Polly. 'Do you know him?'

'Heaven forbid!' said George. 'But you were never out of earshot of one of the boyos, girlo, and we've had some fruity reports. As a matter of fact, Bill Loftus and Bruce Hammond are agog with excitement, you strung him along so well.'

'*Is* he the man?' asked Polly.

'Oh, there's not much doubt about that,' said George. 'He went first to the house of Old Iron Face. There he doubtless received instructions. He's an artist,' he admitted, 'there's no doubt about that. Our subject wasn't mentioned, was it?'

'No.'

'Tomorrow, same time, same place,' said George, with a comical lift of his eyebrows.

She laughed. 'Nearly,' she said.

'Good girl! Are you coming into join the party for an hour, or are you going to sleep it off?'

'I think I'll join the party,' said Polly. They were in the hall at *The Pines*.

'Good! You and I together, I'm the only other member,' said George, and he took her arm and led her into the back garden, where the moon was rising and there was quiet loveliness in the tall, stately trees. 'You see,' said George, 'when I've a mind to it, I can cast the same spell. Hallo, Bill,' he added, as they came across Christine and Bill Loftus, the latter smoking his pipe, sitting in the cool night air near the tennis court. 'Polly's come to report,' he said. 'The pretty gent has staked a claim but hasn't yet tried to work it.'

'Kick him, Polly,' said Christine.

'Or better, ignore him,' said Loftus. 'We've heard a little of how it's been going,' he added, 'and it promises very well. I was right about the velvet glove, thanks be. Did anything else worth reporting happen during the day?'

'Only one thing,' said Polly, and she told them about the strange effect of Hoffmann on her companion.

'Odd,' said Loftus. 'Hoffy will be in soon, and we'll find out whether he recognized your man.'

'The man certainly recognized him,' said Polly.

They went in and joined the others. George entertained the company with some conjuring tricks which made even the quiet Hammond chuckle, and delighted Professor Toller. It occurred to Polly for the first time that the Professor was doing remarkably little work on his newest inventions, but she did not dwell on that. She even forgot that Hoffmann had not returned, and when she went to bed, a little after midnight, she was thinking more about George's antics than of Maurice.

Downstairs, Loftus looked about the lounge. The atmosphere had grown tense since Polly, Christine and two other women—Mike Errol's wife and Guy Grey's fiancée—had retired.

'So we've a job to do tonight,' Loftus was saying. 'Polly is quite sure about Hoffmann, and she wouldn't make a mistake. Obviously he recognized him, but he hasn't reported and hasn't turned up. Something's amiss. Search the streets—I'll get the police busy, too—and go anywhere you think wise, but don't go too near Rutter's house.'

'Rutter?' echoed two or three of the young men.

'Iron Face is known locally as Rutter,' said Loftus.

The police and most of the agents of Department Z searched Bournemouth thoroughly during that moonlit night, but they found no trace of the little Jew. Yet at breakfast next morning all the men seemed fresh and bright, and Hoffmann was not mentioned. Polly asked George what Hoffmann had said when he had come in, and George replied evasively but gave her no cause for alarm.

She left the hotel at ten minutes to eleven.

Maurice was waiting for her by the fountain. He was dressed in a suit which was nearly white, with quarter-inch stripes of many colours, and he looked exquisite. And soon she was sitting in a luxurious easy chair in the sitting-room of Rutter's house, though she did not know it was Rutter's, listening to Maurice playing the piano. He had a light touch, but he was nothing like the player that he seemed to think himself. Then suddenly he stopped, turned and smiled at her, and asked:

'Are you happy at your hotel?'

He nearly caught her unawares, but she recovered and said, with an air of surprise:

'Yes, it's all right.'

'Hotels,' said Maurice, 'are usually unbearable.' He stood up and held out both his hands to her—'we are wasting time! I wonder, now, if I will be forgiven if I ask your name?'

'Dalton,' she said, promptly. 'Polly Dalton.'

'Polly!' echoed Maurice, and nearly made her laugh. Until

then the curious spell which he exerted had remained, but it was broken now. 'I,' he said, 'am Maurice—Maurice Mondelle. Yes! Mondelle! I am French. Did you perceive that?'

'No,' said Polly.

'I had the thrice-blessed good fortune to be born in Paris, of French parents, where I inherited an eye for beauty,' said Maurice, 'and to have an English education. Superb! Let us go in to lunch, my dear; it seemed to me that we would be much happier lunching here, with no one to spoil our enjoyment. Meals at *The Pines*,' he added, with a delicate shudder, 'must be intolerable.'

'Oh, they're not bad,' said Polly.

During lunch he questioned her closely, rarely stringing two questions together but always working them in with his flamboyant talk of other things. She told the story which she had so carefully rehearsed. Some of the guests at *The Pines* seemed to be good friends, but she did not think they all knew one another. She had gone there after she had left the *Mayberry* because she had been a little alarmed by things that had happened at her first hotel. A young man named George had recommended *The Pines*, and he was staying there. He was a rather absurd young man, but quite amusing. Yes, he knew some of the other men—especially an old one named Toller...

By degrees, she told him about the incidents at the *Mayberry*, incidents of which obviously he already knew, and she let it be known that George Henry George was a little tiresome with his attentions. The questions Maurice put, more blatant now, although she did not appear to notice that, grew more and more concerned wih Toller. Did she know when he went out, what he was doing, why he had selected *The Pines* after leaving the *Mayberry*?

'Well,' said Polly, 'he always seems—well, *frightened*.'

'Yes, frightened,' said Maurice, nodding. 'There is not much that you fail to observe, my dear Polly. I have no doubt that the man George has told you some foolish story about *helping* Professor Toller.'

Polly gaped. 'Do you know him?'

'Very well,' said Maurice. '*Very* well. Tell me, Polly, has George or any other men there used the word—the letter—Z?'

Polly said: 'No.' Her instructions about that had been most emphatic, and she thought the answer pleased Maurice. She chose that moment to pretend not to understand why he was so interested, and he gave his superior but very attractive smile, and said:

'I am in Bournemouth with a *mission*.'

'Mission?' echoed Polly.

'I am acting on behalf of Professor Toller's friends,' said Maurice, blandly. 'He is in some danger. Your belief that he is afraid is only too well founded. He believes that George and the others are his friends, but they wish him nothing but harm.' He looked intently at her, and then quickly away. 'But I am worrying you, my dear. You must forgive me. I should not—'

'Please go on,' said Polly, and hated her triteness. No wonder the man thought her a fool.

'You are very good,' said Maurice. 'If I could have five minutes—no more, no less—alone with the Professor, I think I could help him. I wish to give him a message which I cannot trust to others. Will you ask him if he will meet me—shall we say beneath the suspension bridge in Alum Chine, at eleven o'clock tomorrow morning?'

'I suppose I can,' said Polly.

'No one else must hear you,' said Maurice. 'And tell him that Dr. Morritz has sent the message. No, I am not Morritz, I am a friend of his, and a *very* good friend of the Professor's. Will you do it for me, my dear?'

'There's no reason why I shouldn't,' said Polly.

'But *every* reason why you should,' said Maurice. 'And there is another thing, of great importance. If anyone else thought that the Professor was going to meet Dr. Morritz, *anything* might happen. On your oath, Polly, you will tell no one else?'

'Why should I?' she asked.

'I knew that I could rely on you,' said Maurice, and he patted her hand.

The telephone bell rang a few minutes afterwards. He excused himself with punctilious courtesy, went to the telephone in a corner of the room, and, after a word or two, replaced it.

'A friend has called to see me,' he said, 'I will be with you in a very few minutes.' He seemed suddenly alert.

He went out, closing the door.

'After it had closed, there was a faint click. Polly got up, hesitantly, and then moved towards the door and tried the handle. It turned, but the door would not open. Something like panic reared up in her, and she had to bite her lips to prevent herself from uttering a sharp cry. She turned away from the door and looked out of the window. It faced the back garden, and she had already noticed the shrubs and small trees growing there, all clipped and tidy, yet making the garden look overcrowded.

There was a net curtain over the lower half of the window; she could not be seen from outside, but she could see out. She saw a movement among the shrubs, and then a man came into sight—an ugly little man, with a bald head and a patch or two of black hair above his temples. He was bending low, as if hiding from someone else in the shrubbery.

Other shrubs moved.

To Polly Dalton it was an odd, almost weird experience. The little man's movements were undoubtedly furtive—and she caught her breath when she saw what he had in his hand. It was a small gun with a long barrel; a gun small enough to be held with comfort in his hand. He moved the bush aside gently. The bush farther away moved again.

Polly pressed closer to the window.

Then she saw a man dart into sight, and recognized Hoffmann! The little Jew was sideways to her. He was running from one shrub to another, and he was in sight only for a moment. In that moment the man with the gun fired. She heard nothing, but she saw a wisp of smoke and a flash of yellow. She did not know whether Hoffmann was hit. She saw him disappear into the shrubs and the bald-headed man race after him. Others came into sight, two large men and a small fellow whom she remembered having seen in the *Norfolk* when she had dined with George.

Hoffmann came in sight again.

He jumped out of the bushes and clung to the branch of a pine tree. In a moment he was out of sight, hidden by the branches, but the tree was shaking. The men made their way towards it.

The thing that seemed to Polly to be the most uncanny of all was the silence. For the first time she realized that she had not heard a sound of any kind from outside the room.

The tree was shaking as if blown by a high wind.

Then she saw Hoffmann drop from the far side and stand poised for a moment on top of a wall; until that moment the wall had merged with the bushes and trees, and she had not realized it was there. One of the big men came into sight, but Hoffmann disappeared, his arms flung wide. She did not think he was hurt.

She was quite stiff with excitement mingled with fright. It was the tenseness of her nerves which made her turn, she was not conscious of hearing anything. She saw the handle of the door move, and stepped quickly away from the window and turned over the leaves of a music album. She touched one or two notes, idly, unable to concentrate enough to make a tune.

'I am so glad to see you amusing yourself,' said Maurice. 'I was detained longer than I expected.'

'Oh, that's all right,' said Polly. She hoped her voice sounded calm. 'Can you play this?' She smoothed out the album and began to play a minuet. She dared not look at him, she knew that the colour had gone from her cheeks. In desperation she played as she had rarely played before. Maurice drew up beside her. He stood quite still, and she felt that he was staring at her; her cheeks began to burn. Then he turned the page for her, and she went on with new fervour. She played it to the end, then pushed the stool back.

'Enough!' she cried.

'It is *not* enough, my dear,' said Maurice. 'That was superb! You did not tell me that you had such an exquisite touch.'

'Oh, I hardly play at all,' she said. She turned to the window and glanced out, without making any attempt to move towards it. 'It's heavenly out of doors,' she said, 'and rather stuffy in.'

'I know,' said Maurice, resting his hands on her shoulders. 'I wish I could spend the afternoon as I did yesterday, my dear Polly, but unfortunately I have to stay in. Work—work! Always work! You do understand, don't you?'

'Of course,' she said.

'And you will remember the importance of that message?'

'Yes.'

'You are *very* good,' said Maurice.

She got up determinedly and picked up her bag. He insisted on taking her to the end of the street, which led to the cliff road, and before she left him, while he held her hand gently, he said:

'Tomorrow, here—at eleven.'

'All right,' she said.

She had never been more glad to get away from a man, a place, a situation. She stumbled in her eagerness to escape and to get back to *The Pines*—and then she discovered that she had lost her way. The streets seemed all the same, the houses were much alike, even the people who passed her seemed the same. She set her lips and tried again, and then came for the third time upon the same hotel.

From the small garden in front of it spoke a man who was hidden by bushes:

'Don't jump out of your skin. Go straight on, take the first right and the first left—you'll know where you are then.'

She looked at the hotel doubtfully.

'You will,' the man assured her. 'I can't show myself, you're being followed.'

'All right,' she said.

Why all this mystery? she asked herself, as she walked on, taking his first direction. Was it necessary? What had happened to Hoffmann? Was she wise to go on with this? Was there any purpose in it? Could she really believe what Loftus and the others told her? Why did they want a girl to help them? There were a dozen men at least at *The Pines*, she was tired of this hole-and-corner business, the mystery, the danger, the fears which came and went like hot shivers when one was in the grip of fever.

She took the left turn, as she had been told, and at the end of a long, twisting road, she found herself on the top of the cliff. There were crowds of people, most of them lolling in the shade of the pines, a few walking swiftly and laughing together.

'Why, hallo, Miss Dalton,' said Christine Loftus.

Polly started, and turned.

Christine was sitting in a shelter built into the face of the cliff, which just there was higher than the level of the road. She was alone, with a book open on her lap, and she made to get up. She was wearing a cream linen suit, and looked, as always, calm, fresh and composed. By contrast, Polly felt hot and bothered.

'Thank heaven *you're* here,' she said, and sat down next to Christine. 'I just don't think I can go on.'

'Don't talk too loudly,' said Christine. 'Why?'

'That's why!' cried Polly. 'Don't talk too loudly. Don't look over your shoulder, although you know you are being watched. Don't start when voices you don't expect come from behind you. Put up with a scented *pansy* for two whole days, tell lie after lie, bear gladly with fools—I tell you I can't stand it!'

'The surprising thing to me is that you've stood it so well,' said Christine. 'If you knew what is behind it, if you had some personal stake in it, you'd feel much better. They've told you as much as they dare, but it hasn't been enough to satisfy you. I wish I could help.'

'You're a help, just being there,' said Polly. 'I think I've only now realized that you add a note of sanity to the whole crazy business. Everything else seems unreal, even the Professor seems unreal—*is* he a professor?'

'Yes.'

'If these people wish him harm, why don't they shoot him or be done with it quickly?' demanded Polly extravagantly.

Christine laughed. 'They've good reasons for wanting him dead, equally good ones for preventing us from finding out why. Did you learn anything today?'

'Yes. Maurice'—she grimaced—*'that's* the scented pansy's name! He wants him to meet Dr. Morritz beneath the suspension bridge at Alum Chine, tomorrow morning at eleven. I—

Maurice, Morritz,' she. said, suddenly alert. 'They're very much alike in sound, aren't they? Maurice—Morritz. I—' She stopped, stared at Christine, and added in a louder voice: 'What is it? What's the matter? What—'

For suddenly Christine gasped and put a hand to her shoulder. At the same moment two men raced past the entrance to the shelter. Polly stared at them, and recognized Dunster and Grey. Then she looked back at Christine—and beneath Christine's hand she saw something bright red. Blood!

Christine said, quickly: 'Don't worry. Fold up your scarf, please, quickly. In a wad.' She was pressing her hand against her shoulder, near the neck, and the red patch was getting larger. 'Please,' she said. She took the scarf and placed it, folded several times into a tight wad, against her shoulder, before she took her hand away. The palm of her hand was red and glistening with blood.

Polly said: 'You can't walk!'

'I must, as far as the road. Telephone the house and tell them to send a car,' said Christine. She stood up, her lips set tightly, but before she got out of the shelter she swayed. Polly seized her arm and made her sit down, looked round and saw that no one was immediately outside the shelter. Then two lads and a girl passed, hurrying, with strained looks on their faces. She stepped on to the path and saw a crowd gathering a hundred yards along—and, above the crowd, high on the cliff, three men were struggling.

Beneath them, she knew, was a drop of several hundred feet.

8

POLICE FOR POLLY

Dunster and Grey, who had been following Polly, saw the little man with black hair pass the entrance to the shelter, and turn towards it. They saw nothing else, but heard a faint sound—and then the little man gave a quick, frightened glance over his shoulder. He saw them and broke into a run, and in a moment they were after him.

They saw Polly and Christine in the shelter, saw the tension on their faces. Then they concentrated on catching up with the man. Grey, the taller of the two, led the way. The little man threaded between the people, angry shouts were flung at all three as they pushed men and women on one side. The crowd on the cliff top stood and stared.

Dunster kept nearer to the cliff, Grey kept to the other side of the path. Grey was making headway. He drew almost level with his quarry, who glanced at him and then ran towards the cliff edge. There were sand-dunes and tufts of coarse grass, and a few people stood on top of little mounds, overlooking the bay.

In some places there were only a few feet between the path and the cliff edge; at others there were twenty feet or more. At one of the wider stretches the little man left the path. Grey turned after him.

By then Dunster had reached the spot where their quarry—Peel—had run off the path. Peel went up one of the mounds, and then he stopped, for, unexpectedly, he looked down at the side of the cliff, to the motor-road and promenade below. The cliff was steep, but not sheer; it was just possible for a man to climb down.

Peel turned his back on the sea and began to lower himself—and then Dunster reached the mound, flung out a hand and gripped Peel's wrist.

Frightened eyes stared at Dunster; Peel struggled, but could not stop himself from being dragged up. He was on his feet, and he lashed out at Dunster, kicking him on the knee. Dunster lost his grip, wincing.

Grey came up, and grabbed Peel's outflung arm.

Below them, on more level ground, a crowd had collected, a woman was calling 'Police!' and a man was shouting: 'Stop that, you fools, stop that!' No one ventured up the side of the mound until a policeman came up on a bicycle, let it fall and hurried to the struggling men.

Peel, one hand gripped by Dunster, one by Grey, was kicking and struggling, but it looked as if he had lost his chance.

Then the earth gave way beneath them.

A woman screamed; a dog began to bark furiously, others took up the cry. Bedlam reigned. The policeman tried to get to the top of the mound, and then the earth disappeared in front of him, and he jumped back hastily.

Dunster, who had been on a level with the policeman a

moment before, was now almost out of sight. He was gripping the edge of the mound with his hands, and slowly falling lower. He kicked out with his feet. Some sand gave way, but he managed to get a foot-hold. He stood there, with the sand slipping slowly both from his feet and his hands. He looked down...

Far beneath him people were walking along the Undercliff Drive as if at snail's pace. Others dotted the crowded sands and little dots of many colours appeared against the blue water. No one down there knew what was happening higher up.

Nearer Dunster were Grey and Peel, and Grey still had a grip on Peel's arm!

They had lodged on a piece of rock which jutted out, and Grey was holding on to a shrub which grew almost at right angles from the cliff. Peel had his back against a larger rock. His face was distorted, and he was desperate enough even then to kick out at Grey.

He caught the Department man on the knee.

Grey gasped, and his foot slipped.

Dunster saw him lose his grip, try desperately to regain his balance, and then fall slowly backwards. Peel stood staring, as if he could not believe his eyes.

Dunster clung on, his hold precarious, not knowing from one moment to the next whether he would be precipitated in Grey's wake. He saw Grey strike the side of the cliff, bound off, then strike it again. A rubble of stone, sand and dirt fell down, reached the Undercliff Drive, and made people look up in surprise. In a few seconds a sea of faces was strained upwards, and along the edge of the cliff a cordon of people were staring down. Bathers waded from the sea and the beach towards the scene.

Dunster moved one foot, cautiously. There was a stratum

of rock not far away. If he could get to that he would be safer, and might be able to climb down after Grey.

A rope was suddenly flung over the cliff, and a deep voice, from a man who was out of sight, called:

'Hold that if you can.'

'More to the left,' called Dunster.

The rope moved a foot towards him. He stretched out one hand and grabbed it, then said, in a harsh voice:

'Hold it—I'm going down.'

'Don't be a fool!' cried the man with the deep voice—the policeman who had nearly met disaster. 'Don't—'

Dunster said: 'I must go down.'

He looked down again. He could not tell where Grey was, but he saw a shower of rubble flying out from the side of the cliff, with a larger rock which made the crowd below sway and give way. It looked like a convulsion in that sea of upturned faces. People spread out in all directions, like a rapidly opening flower.

'Come *up!*' called the policeman.

Dunster was now looking at Peel. The little man's hat had fallen off and his bald head looked yellow in the sun, the fringe of black hair looked unnatural. He had recovered his balance, and his nerve was remarkable. There was rock a little way from him, and he moved towards it, clinging to the cliff with one hand, stretching out with his leg.

He touched the other rock.

He put his weight on it.

It gave way, and he fell!

The scream which came from his lips as he hurtled down struck a chill of horror in the people lining the cliff top. From the crowd below there came a gargantuan sigh. It floated upwards as Peel hit the side of the cliff, bounced off as Grey had done, and then went down.

* * *

Polly telephoned Bournemouth 81818 from a small hotel near the shelter. She disliked leaving Christine, and the one consolation was that most people were interested only in the scene on the cliff edge.

George answered her.

'George,' she said, 'can you bring a car at once to—to the shelter on the cliff near the *Island View Hotel*. Christine has been hurt.'

'Right,' said George. He rang off with bewildering suddenness, and left her holding the receiver. She hurried back to Christine, who was conscious, but very pale.

'I shall be all right,' she said, 'it's too high to be dangerous. Are they coming?'

'Yes. Mrs. Loftus, you ought to try to get to the hotel across the road. We can bathe the wound, and then—'

'They won't be long,' said Christine. 'I'm better here.'

Within five minutes the whine of a high-powered car sounded near by. The car pulled up silently. Polly darted out of the shelter, and saw George looking about him and Loftus getting clumsily out of the powerful Benz. One of the Errols— Mike, the untidier one—was holding the door open.

'Here!' called Polly.

'What's happening along there?' asked George. The crowd was still getting thicker, everyone out for a walk that afternoon was heading for the throng, which was now seven or eight deep.

'I think—Dunster and that other man, his friend—well, they ran along there, I know that.'

'Oh, Lord!' said George. 'Everything comes at once.' He did not smile, but with Mike Errol and Loftus assisted Christine to the car. No one who saw them could have seen that she had been wounded. Polly did not know by what, for she had heard no sound of a shot.

'In you get, with Christine,' said Loftus to her. Christine was sitting in a corner, and Loftus was sliding into the driving-seat. Polly did as he said, and George closed the door, gave her a smile for the first time that afternoon, and then hurried along to join the crowd.

'*Everything* at once,' he muttered as he reached it.

He made no bones about forcing his way through, elbowing right and left and drawing caustic comments, but looking about him blandly. Almost instinctively he chose the right spot, for when he reached the front Dunster was being hauled over the edge by two policemen and three soldiers, all pulling on the end of a rope. Dunster's eyes were closed, but when he opened them and saw George he said:

'Grey fell over. Get below, will you.'

'Over!' exclaimed George. 'I— All right, old chap.'

He looked in every direction. Fifty yards along was a steep path, but in the cliff, with a few steps cut into the rock at intervals. To the accompaniment of cries of alarm from the nearer people, he climbed over the edge of the cliff and, supporting himself on the top with his arms, he went along, crab fashion, until he reached the path. Then he hurried down. He had the agility of a mountain goat, and paid as little attention to his foothold as a goat would do. He looked towards the left. A light cloud of dust hung over the cliff in places, and a ring of people had gathered about a small, dark object on the Undercliff Drive. He reached the bottom and the ring.

'I think that's a friend of mine,' he said, and the crowd made way for him.

The man he saw was Peel. By some odd chance Peel's face had not suffered badly, but his legs and arms were at peculiar angles from his body, and he had smashed into sharp rock with his chest.

'Is it your friend?' a man asked.

'No, thank God!' said George.

'Don't talk too soon,' chimed in someone else, 'there was two of them.'

Several men were making their way slowly and laboriously up the face of the cliff. George watched them for a few moments, and then saw a man's body, caught against a jutting rock. He did not speak again, but pushed his way through the crowd and began to climb. There was nothing slow or laborious about his rate of progress, and the man on whom he had turned said:

'There'll be a third, if he don't look out.'

George passed a policeman in uniform and two men in khaki. Soon he was higher than any of the rescuers, not more than thirty feet away from Grey. He could not see his friend's face, but he disliked the utter lack of movement. He looked up. The top seemed an infinite distance away.

He reached Grey, and bent over him. Stones and sand were dislodged and went clattering down, while he stood staring. He did not need to touch the body. Guy Grey had not been as fortunate as Peel; he had struck his head upon a rock.

Bill Loftus, quiet, brown Hammond and Hoffmann were with George in the private lounge of *The Pines*. It was early evening of the day of the struggle on the cliff top. Dunster had been put to bed, his body a mass of bruises, and Christine was in a nursing home, where the bullet had been extracted. On the cliff, Peel's gun had been found—one of small calibre, fitted with a rubber silencer. Someone who had been near the shelter at the time had seen him pause, snatch it from his pocket, and point it towards the shelter. Dunster and Grey had also seen that, and had started the chase.

'On a profit and loss,' said Loftus, quietly, 'we are even, at least even. Hoffmann got away, and he's not badly hurt. There's no sign yet that Rutter has decided to move from his house; he may be hoping that Hoffmann didn't recognize it, or else be planning to bluff it out if we go or if the police raid it. Mike Errol, who was watching the house when Polly left, swears that only the little man—his name appears to be Peel— left to follow her. The others were probably hunting the grounds of the houses near by, in the hope of finding Hoffmann.'

'What does it matter?' asked George.

Loftus looked at him woodenly.

'Peel probably had instructions. If Polly were seen with one of us too soon after leaving, to shoot her to prevent her from talking.'

'No,' said George. 'I don't believe that one.'

'He could hardly have been after Christine,' said Loftus.

'Perhaps not,' said George. 'Oh, I don't know. But they wouldn't have let Polly come out only to send a man to shoot her. If they did, the whole business was fantastic.'

'What other motive could Peel have had?' asked Loftus.

Hammond said: 'We've forgotten one thing. Polly admits she was keyed up and talked more freely to Christine than she meant to. If Peel heard her talking, he would know that she was dangerous. That might explain the shot. Dunster says Peel came from the back of the shelter, and then passed the front of it.'

'You've probably got it,' said Loftus. 'Satisfied, George?'

'Better, yes,' said George.

'Now we've got to put the rest of it to the test,' said Loftus.

'The Professor has to be at Alum Chine tomorrow at eleven o'clock. If nothing happens, we'll know that Rutter has seen the red light; if they try to pull anything off, then Polly won that round for us. We know one thing. Rutter has got a man who looks very much like the Professor. Obviously he hopes to spirit our Professor away at Alum Chine, and substitute his.'

'What are we going to do while he's working the trick—have forty winks?' asked George.

'Not quite,' said Loftus. 'We're going to let them have their own way, and get off with our Professor. Surely you've realized the truth about Toller, old chap.'

George, wide-eyed, was obviously at a loss.

'All right, I'll buy it,' he said.

Hammond chuckled, and even Hoffmann smiled, although the Jew did not utter a word; he never uttered a word.

'Our Gabriel Toller is as phoney as Rutter's,' Loftus said. The real Gabriel is safely tucked away, even I don't know where. Our job is to find who is backing Rutter and exactly what is behind it all, but we can't afford to take risks with the real Gabriel.

George opened his mouth wide, backed a pace, and then very slowly smiled—a weak, wan smile, for he had received a shock.

'And I thought it was the genuine article,' he groaned. 'Oh me, oh my. Let me hand in my cards. I'm not cut out for this department. I like my work straightforward.'

Loftus laughed. 'You'll live to learn! Now, I—'

He broke off, for the door opened abruptly, and into the room, her head held high and her hands clenched, marched Polly. An angry Polly, and yet one who was obviously bewildered, distressed and greatly troubled. Anger was uppermost, however; she strode across the room amidst a startled silence, stood in front of Loftus, and said:

'I am *not* going to stand it any longer! So this man here *isn't* Gabriel Toller. It is all a fairy-tale. That card George showed me isn't worth tuppence. All right! I've telephoned the police and asked them to come here at once.'

'Did you say you have, or are going to?' asked Loftus, after a brief pause.

'I have done,' said Polly defiantly. 'The police are on their way,' she paused, puzzled, even disappointed, at the lack of sensation which her announcement caused. George looked rueful and pulled the lobe of his right ear. Bruce Hammond smiled and ran his fingers over the clipped moustache, Loftus looked wooden and quite unimpressed. The trouble with these men was that you could never judge their thoughts from their expressions.

Then she looked at Hoffmann.

He was staring at her, and although his lips were compressed in what might have been a smile, making his nose and chin almost meet, there was reproach in his eyes—the eyes of a man who was gravely hurt.

'Why did you ask them to come?' asked Loftus. 'I mean, what did you tell them we had done?'

'I said you could explain the tragedy on the cliffs,' said Polly.

Loftus looked relieved. 'Oh, that's all right.'

'It *isn't* all right,' said Polly, and she had to fight hard to speak calmly; these men were so wearing down her nerves. 'Nothing is all right. You sit there as if nothing had happened and talk of profit and loss when your own wife has been injured! Mr. Hoffmann was fired at this afternoon, he nearly lost his life, and what have you done about it? Nothing! You say that the Professor is in grave danger, that he isn't the Professor—I mean, you say he might be killed. These people have already tried to kill him *once*, to my knowledge, and yet

79

you propose to send him to be taken prisoner by them. You know they will almost certainly kill him. He may not be the real Professor, but he's a man, he wants to live.'

'Yes, we all want to live,' said Loftus, 'but—'

'No buts can explain this madness!' cried Polly. She turned on Hoffmann, her eyes blazing. 'Were you nearly killed or weren't you?'

Hoffmann nodded; he never seemed to speak, he was so quiet and retiring, and his eyes were filled with such sadness. Now, he smiled at her, reassuringly.

'Then in heaven's name, *why?*' demanded Polly.

'That's one of the things we don't yet know,' said Loftus, 'except that Hoffy recognized Maurice Mondelle as a man he has seen somewhere. He can't recall where. Hoffy's memory isn't good about one period in his life.'

Polly gulped.

'Probably he saw Maurice during that period, and Maurice is afraid that he will be endangered by his evidence,' said Loftus, carefully. 'Maurice and the whole bunch of them are dangerous criminals, you know.'

'Then why don't you report to the police and have them all arrested? I've told you the address. And I shall tell the police, when they arrive,' declared Polly.

'That's all right,' said Loftus. 'When they arrive I think they'll put your mind at rest. Everyone who is working in this affair is a volunteer,' Loftus went on. 'There's no compulsion. Our Professor—let's give him his own name, Bannister— knows the risk he is taking.

'Yet there are some odd facts. George told you the truth when he said that there have been a number of attempts on Professor Gabriel Toller's life, but *all have missed.* The question we ask ourselves is—why?'

'Well, why?' asked Polly.

'Possibly because the assailants meant to miss, but wanted us to think that he was in danger of losing his life,' said Loftus. 'Now they have brought from the Midlands a well-known character actor who has a bad reputation with the police. He has a police record, in fact. They want to exchange him for the man they think is Professor Toller. They wouldn't go to the trouble of making a man look like the Professor if they intended to commit murder and wanted nothing else. Until we knew of this attempt at impersonation, we didn't know that they wanted to kidnap Toller. We do now. That's how we work. Many things happen, mystifying and mysterious. Some are relevant, some don't matter. We sift them thoroughly, try a dozen different ways of looking at the same one, and eventually pertinent facts are thrown up. You see?'

'I'm beginning to see,' said Polly, slowly, 'but—who *are* you?'

Before Loftus could answer there was a tap at the door. Mike Errol ushered in a tall, well-dressed man with a ready smile. He was very fair, and had a remarkably fresh complexion.

'Nice of you to come in person, Superintendent,' said Loftus, removing his arm from Polly's shoulder and shaking hands with the newcomer. 'Miss Dalton, this is Superintendent Carr, of the Bournemouth Police.' He smiled broadly. 'Miss Dalton will probably want evidence that you *are* a policeman!'

Carr smiled. 'That won't be very difficult.' He looked curiously at Polly, and took out his wallet. 'I came myself when we had Miss Dalton's call, because I thought it wiser not to leave this job to others.'

'You're very good,' said Loftus. 'I wish all local police would be as obliging.'

Carr showed Polly a folded card, with his photograph and

details of his position in the Hampshire Constabulary—convincing proof, if the fact that he had come in response to her telephone call were not proof enough. His obvious respect for Loftus set her fears at rest.

Later George led the way out.

'The last thing we expected was that attack on Christine—or on you,' he said. 'You know it might have been intended for you, I suppose?'

'Yes,' said Polly. 'It might have been. Do you think it was?'

'I don't, personally,' said George. 'I think it was meant for Christine. It's the kind of thing that happens to us. Loftus is a terror, you know, and these people have more reason to fear him than anyone of our party—unless Hammond worries 'em most.'

'Hammond's so quiet,' said Polly.

'Yes,' said George. 'He's quiet now.'

Something in his tone made her look at him sharply. She saw a different George, and in his eyes was an expression which reminded her vividly of Hoffmann. They walked about the garden in silence for a while, before she asked:

'Why are you looking like that?'

George said: 'Polly, affairs like this crop up from time to time. The last one was three months ago. I wasn't really in it, I played only a small part. But I had one spot of bad luck. Hammond was the most active worker in the show, Loftus was on leave. I was following a man whom we knew to be involved in a conspiracy of some magnitude. He killed Hammond's wife. It was sudden, something like the attack on Christine. It happened before I could do anything, no one could have saved her. I got the man,' he added, gently. 'He was hanged a month ago, but that didn't help Hammond.'

Polly could not find words.

'It's possible to get used to such conditions,' said George.

'One either cracks up or lives a normal life. To us—I ought to say to the others, I'm such a newcomer—this *is* a normal life. You've noticed that Loftus is weak on his pins, haven't you?'

'Yes.' Her voice was low.

'He lost his leg in one of these shows,' said George, 'and he was lucky not to lose his life. He met Christine during it. Then there's Hoffmann—' He paused, and she looked at him again and saw that his eyes were very hard.

'Yes,' she said, almost inaudibly.

He was in Paris, working for the Department, when the Huns marched in,' said George. 'They didn't know what he was, except that he was a Jew. Just because he is a Jew he has those scars on his cheek. He has other scars on his body. And—they took away his tongue.'

Polly gasped: 'His—*tongue*!'

George went on: 'And afterwards, when he had recovered enough to think, he remembered the job he had been sent to Paris to do. His memory is quite blank for the period when he was in a concentration camp, but he remembers everything before and since that. He escaped from the camp with the help of the F.F.I. He finished his job, escaped to England, and reported. Then he went on working again.'

'It's...' began Polly, and then her voice trailed off.

'Incredible?' murmured George. 'Yes. It makes me think, sometimes! Listen—this isn't a declaration of life-long love. All the same, I've grown attached to you. Call it puppy-love. And I don't want you to stop the next bullet. Go away, Polly, will you?'

She did not answer.

'You've done your job and you've done it well,' said George. 'Maurice, I think, was quite taken in. The very fact that you stuck his company for so long deserves a prize. Go to some other resort. A grateful country will instal you in the finest hotel, and money needn't worry you. Well, what about it?'

They were silent for a long time, and then Polly asked in a small voice:

'That's all very well, but—isn't there any way I can help?'

9

GORDON CRAIGIE

'The girl,' read Loftus's report to London, *'is willing to help, and reluctant to leave Bournemouth. She has been told fully of the dangers, but insists that she wishes to help. I think we can use her. Have you any objection?'*

Gordon Craigie, who had read the long report from beginning to end several times, read the last sentences again, then pushed his chair back from his desk. He walked across the long room towards the fireplace. In spite of the warmth of the day a small coal fire burned in it. He stirred the coals with a poker, and as he did so the bowl of the meerschaum pipe which drooped from his lips nearly touched the top bar. He finished poking and held his thin, pale hands before the little blaze. Then he stood up and rubbed his hands together.

Many people thought Gordon Craigie a cold individual. Physically, he certainly was.

For many years he had spent most of his time in this Whitehall office, and except that there were now three desks where once there had been one, and five armchairs where there had been two, the room looked very much as it had done when Department Z had first come into existence.

In all those years Craigie had altered very little.

His hair was thin on top, and there were growing signs of a bald patch. His eyes looked very tired—but he always looked tired, because his lids dropped so low, making him seem half asleep. His thin, pale face was deeply lined, but the lines gave him a droll, humorous expression. He had taken to wearing *pince-nez*, which served to emphasize the high bridge of his thin, prominent nose.

He was a man of medium height. Recently he had lost weight, although he had never been too heavy. His well-cut clothes were rather loose on the shoulders and about the waist.

The fireplace end of the office had something of the look of a bachelor's den. The armchairs, all very comfortable, were grouped round the fire. On a table near Craigie's chair, which had its back to the window, was a small radio set, a tobacco jar and other oddments, including well-thumbed books.

On the wall within his reach was a pipe-rack, holding six meerschaums. On the fine wooden mantelpiece, beneath the shelf, were several little glass buttons which looked like decorations.

All these things took up about a third of the room, the part being cluttered and untidy but comfortable. The rest of the room was scrupulously tidy. Three steel desks, a dozen steel filing-cabinets, telephones by the dozen—there were in fact, seven on each of two desks and twelve on Craigie's—a dictaphone, several office chairs, and a hat-stand, were all severely practical.

As Craigie sat back in his armchair and began to refill his pipe, he was thinking of the report that had come by hand from Bournemouth late that afternoon, and the description of the girl—Ethel (Polly) Dalton. He had already seen a report about her ordinary life, and he found it difficult to imagine a background less suited to such work as the Department's. Suitability, however, had little to do with background, much to do with adaptability and cold courage. Apparently the girl had these in good measure. Craigie got the impression of a girl somewhat puzzled, even bewildered at times, often out of her depth, but showing surprising resilience.

Loftus would not say that he could use her services unless he felt sure that she would serve a purpose. Craigie had to decide whether he was justified in allowing her to accept the risks involved. People did not really understand those risks at first, or even at second sight.

His pipe was going well when a green light showed in the mantelpiece; it was one of the ornamental glass buttons. Craigie leaned forward and pressed a bell-push just above the button, one that was hidden by the mantelshelf.

The wall next to the mantelpiece opened slowly. Beyond the opening was a cold stone passage leading to grey stone steps. Outlined against it stood a burly, carelessly-dressed man, rather more than middle-aged, powerful-looking, with a florid face. He smiled at Craigie, who started to get up.

'Don't worry, Craigie,' he said. He stepped through, and the door closed behind him without a sound. 'I suppose you've often been asked why you insist on these precautions,' he added, and nodded towards the sliding door.

Craigie smiled. 'Yes. Puerile, aren't they? The answer is that they work—no one has yet forced a way in here.'

'It keeps out more than active enemies,' said the newcomer. He was Gilbert Leven, the Foreign Secretary. His manner was always a little gruff, his smile rather grim; his brown eyes were ready to smile but often held a sober gleam.

'It saves me from being pestered with social calls and convivial visitors,' said Craigie.

Leven laughed. 'You have enough conviviality from your men!'

'They're all right,' said Craigie.

'Yes. I've often thought,' said Leven, sitting down opposite Craigie and taking out his cigarette-case, 'that they put up their façade of facetiousness as a kind of self-defence.'

'In danger some men swear, some pray, mine play the fool,' said Craigie. 'If they didn't, they would probably go raving mad! I sit back here, you know, day after day, rarely going out, and I read the reports of what they do and how they behave in this danger or under that threat, and—well,' said Craigie, 'I've been guiding their activities for more years than I care to think of, and it still amazes me.'

Are there many of the original members left?' asked Leven. He seemed in no hurry; yet he was a man of action and bustle, who seldom rested. He had certainly not come for a social chat or from a point of interest; he would broach his subject when he was ready for it.

Craigie said: 'I started with nine members. Three are still alive. I've several dozen newer men. Five years is a long life for them.'

Leven was quiet for a moment, and then asked: 'How are things going in Bournemouth?'

'Fairly well, I think,' said Craigie. 'There's been much more activity since Bannister became the Professor. There is a plot to kidnap him tomorrow morning.'

Leven stared. 'Tomorrow? How do you know?'

Craigie said: 'A rather unusual temporary worker for us discovered enough to be able to tell Loftus what these people are going to attempt. We'll see what happens after they've got Bannister.'

'You'll let them take him?' asked Leven.

'I don't see what else I can do,' said Craigie. 'It's being worked very neatly. They're going to pass off another man as the Professor, thinking he's in exchange for the real thing. Our man is Bannister—have you met him?'

'Once, I believe,' said Leven.

'He might pick up a few odds and ends for us,' said Craigie. He might have added: 'Or he might not live to tell us anything.' 'Is Toller all right?'

'Yes, and very busy,' said Leven. He threw his cigarette-end into the fireplace, and leaned forward, looking into the red embers. He had a trick of stillness. 'The Prime Minister has gone to Paris,' he added. 'Otherwise he would have been here himself.'

Craigie nodded.

'Professor Toller was working in collaboration with Dr. Morritz,' Leven said, 'but of course you know that.'

'Yes,' said Craigie, 'and so do the people in Bournemouth. They used Morritz's name to persuade our Professor to make an appointment for tomorrow morning.'

'I wonder what these people who've gone to Bournemouth *do* know,' murmured the Foreign Secretary, very softly. 'Too much for my peace of mind, I fancy.'

'And for mine,' said Craigie.

The Foreign Secretary got a little closer to the fire, as if he, as well as Craigie, were cold, and wanted the added warmth. Craigie could only see his profile. There was no smile on it, only a set expression which in itself indicated the gravity of his thoughts.

Leven spoke as if to himself.

'Toller and Morritz were working in collaboration when Morritz disappeared in Paris. The same day there was an unsuccessful attempt to kidnap Toller. It was foiled only by his presence of mind. Yes. The subsequent attacks on Toller's life made us consult you about it. That is—how long ago?'

'Seven weeks,' said Craigie.

'In those seven weeks you have discovered that the man known as Rutter is partly responsible,' said Leven. 'You are, I suppose, quite sure that Rutter is not the principal?'

'Yes,' said Craigie. 'Rutter, also known as Forbeson, is administrative, not executive. He receives instructions. He has worked for other people, sometimes in cases in which we have been involved, but we have never before had him in the position where he is now—we could detain him tomorrow, and with evidence to hang him.'

'Yet he has always been so careful in the past,' said Leven. 'This time he has taken an active part in the affair, taking risks which he has always avoided before. That is some measure of its importance to him.'

'Or the money he'll get for his work,' said Craigie.

'Yes,' said Leven. He looked up with an unexpectedly bright smile. 'And now he wants Toller. Have you discussed the motives behind the affair with your men?'

'With Loftus and Hammond, but not with any of the others,' said Craigie. 'There's no need to, at this juncture. And we're not clear enough about motives. Toller and Morritz were working together on—' He paused.

'T.N.25,' murmured Leven.

'T.N.25,' said Craigie.

They were silent again, and the room seemed very cold. Neither man moved; the symbol seemed to float about the room and echo from the ceiling and the corners. *T.N.25. T.N.25. T.N.25.*

'There are times,' said Leven, with another unexpected smile, 'when I wish the Chinese had never invented gunpowder!'

'Yes,' murmured Craigie.

'T.N.25,' murmured Leven. 'A single cupful would cause as much havoc as a V.2 rocket or a 10-ton bomb. It's simple to make, I'm told. A devil's companion for the atomic bomb. In its way it's as bad. No one knew of this before. Pure chance brought Toller and Morritz together, and they discovered that they were working on almost identical formulæ. Neither worked with assistants who knew what was being prepared, and yet their researches have obviously become known. Yet we and the French have done our best to keep it a closely guarded secret until it is finished and the explosive proves its worth.'

'Yes,' said Craigie.

'Do you know what we propose to do when it *has* proved its worth?' asked Leven.

'I know what I hope we're going to do.'

'What is that?'

'Share it with the other Great Powers,' said Craigie.

'The United Nations,' murmured Leven. 'Yes. You know what we fear, don't you?'

'That Russian agents are after T.N.25.'

'A hateful possibility,' said Leven, 'but we must know for certain. Who else would seek it?'

Craigie did a rare thing; he laughed.

'Now answer yourself,' he said, and Leven smiled.

'There are still Nazis in existence.'

'And Fascists and Japanese,' said Craigie. 'Also, I have seen too much of the activities of private armaments manufacturers to leave them out of count. It may be that we are now dealing with private individuals, wealthy, intent on getting T.N.25 for what it is worth commercially. More dividends on death,' he added, and there was bitterness in his smile. 'Am I offending you?'

'You know you are not,' said Leven.

Craigie said, slowly: 'I do not believe that there is in this country at the present time a single agent of any country, friendly or hostile, with the money, power and freedom of movement to be behind this thing. I am convinced that we have to look nearer home. And'—he looked evenly at Leven— 'I have had a report, only this afternoon, about five men who might be implicated.'

'Ah,' said Leven.

'Five men, each of whom controls large armament concerns,' said Craigie. 'One French, one American—both with English agents—and three English. With each of those five men, Rutter has been known to associate within the last twelve months. I believe that Rutter first discovered the existence of T.N.25, that he sold his knowledge to the highest bidder, and is now selling his services.'

'You sound very certain,' said Leven.

'I feel certain,' said Craigie.

'Who are the five?'

'I would rather wait for a few days,' said Craigie. 'I may be able to delete the names of one or two.'

'I see,' murmured Leven. 'They would shock us?'

'Very much.'

Leven smiled. 'I don't see why I should try to make you alter your usual habits, Craigie! The Prime Minister will be back on Monday, though, and I don't think he will be quite so willing to leave it to you.'

'I might know more by Monday,' said Craigie.

'Yes, of course.' Leven looked at his watch, stood up and smiled. 'I must go, I've several appointments this evening. Who else knows those five names?'

'Loftus and Hammond,' said Craigie. 'And there is a curious thing, which makes me believe that this has been going on longer than we realized. Hammond's wife was murdered three months ago. Early this afternoon an attack was made on Loftus's wife. It failed, although she was injured. In every case where Rutter has worked—or where I believe he has worked—there has always been a tendency to indirect attack. We have evidence that many of the Department men are known to Rutter, but not a single attack has been made on any of them. Several have been made on their wives. It may be an attempt to blackmail them into working less thoroughly.'

'Your Mr. Rutter, then, has a lot to learn,' said Leven. 'Good-bye, Craigie. Thanks.' He shook hands, his grip powerful, and went to the door. When Craigie had his finger on the opening button, Leven turned and looked at him. 'We must find the truth of it. Morritz knows the secret and might be forced to give it away.'

'According to Professor Toller,' said Craigie, 'Morritz knows the theory, only Toller has yet succeeded in finding a way to make T.N.25 a commercial proposition. While we keep Toller safe, we haven't too much to fear.'

After Leven had gone, Craigie went to his desk, took a memorandum-pad, and wrote swiftly. He used an abbreviated longhand, which few people could decipher, and wrote in code. After five minutes at the desk he tore off a sheet of paper and put it in an envelope, which he stuck down but did not otherwise seal.

The last sentence was: *Use Miss Dalton in any way you think will serve.*

10

BENEATH THE BRIDGE

Bannister left *The Pines* at half-past ten.

He was alone, and he walked with long, easy strides, yet nothing about him suggested that he was nearer thirty than seventy. He carried a gnarled walking-stick, was dressed in shabby flannels and a Norfolk jacket, and wore a battered trilby hat.

The beach was not yet overcrowded, but there were hundreds of people, whole families settling down for the day, a few early arrivals already bathing. Large, complex sand-castles were being built by earnest youngsters, small sand-castles being built by earnest infants.

Past all this Bannister strode, smiling about him.

He might be going to his death.

He knew that as well as the Errols and Hoffmann, who followed him.

Hoffmann did not look very much like Hoffmann, in spite of his nose and chin. His cheeks looked plumper, his thin body was filled out, he walked with a stick. He was dressed as a woman—a middle-aged woman with heavy tread. The Errols looked like—the Errols. They were in close attendance on Bannister, and they knew quite well that at least one of Rutter's men was following them.

As they drew near Alum Chine, fewer people were about. Bannister reached the path which ran through the chine to the residential streets on higher ground. From the sea-shore to the streets, along that path, it was a walk of twenty minutes at average walking pace. When Bannister had been walking for five minutes, however, the scene had changed. Wooded land was on either side of him, a glory of beech and birch, fern and long grass. The banks were rugged. Here and there steps were cut in them leading to roads on the right-hand side.

Bannister strode on purposefully. There were iron railings on one side of the path, but on the other common land, some sandy, some grass-covered. A few children played there, dogs chased other dogs or their own tails, a few seats were occupied by elderly people, already tired because the path ran uphill.

Suddenly Bannister moved off the path, and in a moment he was hidden from sight. Behind him, Mike Errol stopped.

Mark said, in a surprisingly loud voice:

'Where the dickens has he gone?'

'Towards those steps, perhaps,' said Mike.

'Possibly. The old idiot,' grumbled Mark. 'Why the devil we don't put him in irons is beyond me. He's nothing but a nuisance. A walk—phaugh!'

'Hold it,' said Mike. 'The old chap must have some fresh air.'

'I wish he'd choose somewhere else,' said Mark.

All this was for the benefit of a big man, dressed in a sailor's jersey and serge trousers, who was doing something with a rope at the side of the chine. He had red hair, and was freshly shaved. He heard every word, although he did not appear to pay attention.

'I'll go to the steps,' said Mark.

'I'll keep my eyes open,' said Mike. 'He's probably gone to commune with nature.'

'We'll have to commune with Loftus if we lose him,' said Mark darkly.

All this had been prearranged; its purpose was simply to make any of Rutter's men within earshot believe that they thought the Professor had come out for a morning stroll, and that they were perturbed only because he had given them the slip. They began to search, but did not find him, and, when Mike was searching with visible anxiety among the thickets, the man with red hair stood upright and raised his hand above his head.

A plump Jewess, now walking with heavier step, passed him as he did so. The red-haired man did not spare Hoffmann a second glance.

Farther along the chine, almost immediately beneath the suspension bridge, was little Lodge, rather scared, hopping from one foot to the other. Directly he got the signal from the first of Rutter's men, he turned and hurried into the trees. Just there the foliage was very thick. Somewhere out of sight a brook gurgled softly. A few yards farther away from the sea, the flat boards of the suspension bridge, all that was visible from the path, boomed and echoed as people walked across.

Bannister, who had gone straight towards the bridge, knowing that the Errols would 'lose' him, peered towards the path from behind an oak tree. No one was near. He saw little, pimply Lodge disappear into a thicket, and after a few moments the man reappeared.

Maurice was with him, elegant and very alert.

'Toller's about somewhere,' Lodge said. 'I saw him. Where's Kelly?'

'Don't give him a name, you fool,' said Maurice. 'He's all ready.'

Bannister saw them talking. Maurice walked from the path towards the steps cut in the bank, looking about him warily. Bannister suddenly appeared from behind the tree, and Maurice stopped in his tracks.

'Why Professor!' he said.

'Who are you?' demanded Bannister. His inflection was remarkably good, the sonorous voice, learned from gramophone records after much practice, was exactly like Toller's. He looked at Maurice with a frown, and pretended not to notice Lodge. Two other men from Rutter were now within sight, but could not be seen from the path.

For Bannister, it was the crucial moment.

For the Errols, pretending to look the other way but aware of what was happening, it was a moment of great tension. For Hoffmann, now admiring some large ferns near the railings on the path, it was a moment which made his heart beat so fast that it almost suffocated him.

Rutter might want Toller; but he might be intent only on substituting his masquerader. There was no certainty that Bannister would be taken alive, but a real possibility that, once Kelly had been 'found' by the Errols, he would be shot; he might even be shot before that.

Bannister looked into Maurice's smiling eyes.

Lodge drew nearer; so did the other two men. He of the red hair had left his rope and was walking along the path. Dozens of people were sauntering along it, a few children were playing within a hundred feet of the scene—and Bannister did not move, but only frowned and waited for

Maurice to speak again, or for a shot which he might not hear but which might send him to eternity.

'I have a message for you, my dear Professor,' said Maurice, and there was a sneer on his face which made him look no longer handsome. 'From Dr. Morritz.'

'I was told of that,' said Bannister. 'What is it?'

'I will tell you in a few moments,' said Maurice.

'What do you mean, sir? Either you have a message for me, or you are telling lies.' During that little speech Bannister looked in all directions, as if it were dawning on him that this was a trick, that he should not have evaded the Errols. 'Let me have you know, sir, that I am with friends—'

'Whom you very neatly dodged,' said Maurice. 'Don't worry, Professor, your friends—'

He also broke off on that word. Lodge, who had been sidling nearer to Bannister, suddenly stepped forward. Something glinted in his hand. Involuntarily Bannister swung round towards him, trying to strike the glittering thing away. Maurice stepped forward and clapped a hand over his mouth, then gripped Bannister's right arm.

A needle point was driven into Bannister's arm.

'All right!' cried Lodge, exultantly. 'He's got the full dose. All right!'

He withdrew the glittering thing, a hypodermic syringe, and thrust it into his pocket. Bannister had not moved; and there was fear in him, for he did not know what the needle had contained, did not know what drug was even then circulating through his body. Suddenly he made a convulsive effort, and succeeded in breaking away. He stumbled over the root of a tree and pitched forward.

As he fell, Lodge struck him behind the head with a short ebony ruler. Bannister plunged into long grass. Maurice, swinging round, surveyed the path. No one was looking towards them— except a plump Jewess, half hidden by the trees, who was sitting on a seat smoking a cigarette. She got up.

Bannister lay there unconscious, hidden from everyone except Maurice and his men, who were close by. One of them hurried towards the thicket where Maurice had been hiding, and disappeared. The red-haired man came up, and Maurice said:

'Get him out of sight.'

'Okay.' Bannister was no light-weight but, taking advantage of the foliage of the small trees, the red-haired man raised him, grunted as he hoisted him to his shoulder and then, in a dozen strides, was safely hidden from all prying eyes.

The Errols, a hundred yards apart from each other, saw little of that; but they had seen Bannister go down. Their hearts were heavy within them, although it was what they had expected. The uncertainty was the thing which worried them most, not knowing whether Bannister was alive or dead.

Five minutes later from the first thicket came a man who looked like Professor Toller.

Mark whistled; Mike rubbed the end of his nose.

The likeness to Toller—and Bannister when disguised— was uncanny. Rutter even appeared to have found an old Norfolk jacket, shabby flannels and a battered hat, which looked like Bannister's. They *were* Bannister's; in those few minutes his top clothes had been stripped from him, two men were putting others on him.

Rutter's Kelly did not appear to see Maurice or any of the others. He showed great interest in a tiny growth on the trunk of a small oak, and seemed absorbed in that. Maurice, Lodge, the red-haired man and all the party withdrew to the safety of the trees. The little Jewess threw away her cigarette and began to walk up the chine again.

On the suspension bridge, looking down, stood Rutter. He was smiling now, with the reluctant curve of his lips which was his nearest approach to expressing satisfaction.

The Errols descended upon Kelly, who knew them by sight and gave a vacant smile. Kelly was probably the most nervous man in Bournemouth at that moment.

'You put the wind up us,' said Mark.

'We've been hunting high and low,' said Mike reprovingly. 'Did you have to dodge off like that?'

'My dear fellow,' said Kelly, his voice a little high-pitched. He coughed, and spoke on a lower tone. It was too low. He tried again, watching the Errols closely, but they gave no sign that the voice sounded strange, and Kelly regained a little confidence.

'My dear fellow, I was attracted by a rare specimen of parasite. I am surely at liberty to examine such things more closely if I wish?'

'Do it with us,' urged Mike.

'Won't *any*thing make you understand that you're in danger?' demanded Mark.

Kelly coughed again, and turned away.

'Nonsense,' he said, testily. 'Nonsense! You exaggerate. I have always told you that you exaggerate. I— Look! Look at that! An even finer specimen!' He scrambled up the bank with the agility of a young man, and behind his back the Errols exchanged winks.

They too felt better.

It was not wise to dwell too much on Bannister.

Loftus and Hammond were sitting alone in the small sitting-room. It was early evening. Upstairs Kelly, who played his part well, was 'resting'. He had returned from the walk and complained of a headache, had his meals in his room, and was obviously taking as many precautions against discovery as he could.

Bannister had completely disappeared with Maurice and the others. The woods on either side of the chine had been carefully but surreptitiously searched by plain-clothes police as well as by Department Z men, but no trace had been found. There was some satisfaction to be derived from the fact that there was no body; that was the limit of the reassuring results.

'I've come across some odd shows,' said Loftus, 'but this beats the band. *They just didn't leave the chine.*'

'I suppose they could have climbed up the banks,' said Hammond, reasonably.

'We had every hundred yards watched. If they'd come up from the chine in ones or twos, or altogether, we would have seen them. There wasn't a stretch of the road which we hadn't under surveillance—but then, you know that as well as I do,' said Loftus, a little irritably. 'There were six men in all—Bannister, and he was unconscious if not dead, Maurice, the red-head, the little man with the pimply face and a brace of others. They all disappeared.'

Since midday Loftus and Hammond had been severely shaken. Not only had Rutter's men disappeared from Alum Chine, leaving no trace of their going, but the whole Rutter household had moved. They had not gone back to the house and, in the early afternoon, the fire service had received an urgent call from a neighbour. It arrived at the house too late to do anything to help, for the inside was an inferno. They saved other houses near by, although being in its own grounds, Rutter's house burned without endangering much other property. The grounds were blackened and scorched, and there was no trace of contents or residents. Rutter, Bannister and the others had disappeared into thin air.

'They'll probably try to get out of the chine tonight,' said Hammond. 'You know, Bill, it wouldn't be impossible to dig a hole or two, cover it with bracken, and hide there for a while. After dark, all they have to do is to pop out and climb up the banks. We'd better take precautions against that.'

'Yes,' said Loftus, and lifted the telephone. 'It's a good thing that Carr is helpful.'

Superintendent Carr, whom he telephoned, was still helpful and willing. Loftus told him briefly what he wanted. The whole of Alum Chine was to be watched, and car head-lamps were to be shone on the roads at the top, along the path, and on the banks.

'You'll need more than car headlamps,' said Carr. 'I think I can find a firm who will start work at once, and get the whole chine floodlit.'

By half-past six workmen were in Alum Chine and on the banks, fixing cables to carry the power to light the flood-lamps. People gathered and watched them. The residents were curious, but holiday-makers outnumbered them by ten to one. At half-past eight the crowd was thick, and thousands thronged the chine and the surrounding district. Special forces of the police were called. The chine, after a long, weari-some effort, was cleared of all but police and Department Z men, and so were the roads which looked down on it. Men were stationed at every flight of steps, and at every place where the bank was negotiable.

When darkness fell, thousands of people were still near by, harassing the police, occasionally breaking the ropes which cordoned off the chine. There was a constant rumble of conversation and an occasional laugh. A little boy, no more than seven, escaped from his parents and darted laughingly across the road. He was near Mark Errol, who dived and saved him from falling over the edge.

Then the lights went on.

The scene was remarkable, not easily to be forgotten. The chine became alive. Trees were lighted up, casting odd shadows; there were patches of shadow and patches of bright light. Policemen walking along the path could be seen clearly. The crowd murmured at first, because the blaze of light dazzled them, and then gave way to silent wonder. Loftus and the little party with him watched, not unaffected by the magic of the scene.

In the strange quiet the ripple of the sea against the beach was audible, a soft lullaby.

Polly said to George: 'They won't get through *this*.'

'Let's hope,' said George. He was more nervous than usual, and he smoked cigarettes chain-fashion. 'I wouldn't like to be too sure. I'm not even sure the beggars are there. I—'

He broke off with an exclamation. It was taken up by everyone else, for there was a dull, rumbling roar not far away—as if there had been an explosion in the chine. Then, like a shrill chorus from a thousand throats, there came a scream.

Part of the steep bank began to cave in, and with it went many of the people.

11

LANDSLIDE

After the first great cry of alarm and fear, all sound of human voices was drowned by the deep, rumbling roar of falling earth. Out of sight of Polly, George and the party with them, a stretch of the chine moved downwards, carrying helpless people with it. As the landslide grew in extent and speed, as more earth was shaken loose and began its sluggish fall, panic spread like lightning among the people.

Those who had been near the edge, were gone.

Some cooler spirits tried to stem the tide, but the great majority turned and fought and kicked and ran in the desperate effort to get away from danger. While the rumbling of the landslide filled the air and spread alarm much farther afield, that panic grew. Faces illuminated in the garish light of the huge lamps were distorted, terror showed on white, strained faces, glaring eyes seemed feverish in the brightness.

Here and there a man or woman went down in the stampede, and over them rushed the others.

Polly saw it all.

She also saw Loftus bend down and speak close to

George's ear. Superintendent Carr had already gone forward, for the fall had been on their side, and now the crying, struggling mass of people was getting nearer, the leaders of the stampede were already abreast. She saw three terrified girls, gaily dressed in holiday clothes, forced slowly towards the edge of the chine, and she saw their open mouths and eyes filled with terror, as, remorselessly, the crowd pushed them nearer disaster.

One disappeared.

'George!' cried Polly. 'Can't you—'

The rumbling noise had lessened and the shrieking was audible now, drowning her own cry. George gripped her arm and put his mouth close to her ear.

'Orders to stop here!' he bellowed.

A second girl disappeared over the edge, arms and legs waving. Polly darted forward, but George caught her hand. She pulled against him for a moment, then realized that he was right to stop her, and went back. The third woman flung herself into the crowd and was lost among it, while her companions were somewhere over the edge, possibly safe against a tree or shrub, perhaps still falling.

Then Polly saw Loftus, the Errols, Carr and several other members of Department Z, and for the first time she heard a voice clearly. Loftus was shouting, and his voice was incredibly loud. He moved as if both legs were his own, and now he stretched out his hands. Carr and the others joined hands, making a barrier of human flesh across the road. A few people escaped the barrier and went flying past, to stop a little farther away, gasping for breath and beginning to feel the first twinge of shame.

Other men, strangers from the crowd, joined Loftus and his party.

Loftus was roaring:

'Stop where you are. Stand still! Stand still!'

He kept on bellowing, and the words became a refrain. As he shouted men and women rushed at him, unable to stop themselves because of the pressure from behind, but they came against a body as massive as a wall, and got no farther.

The pressure grew worse.

Loftus, still booming out the warning, still heard above the noise of panic, felt the strain of the weight against him and gave way an inch at a time. The others resisted with the same grim determination. If the stampede were allowed to continue, none knew how many people would be crushed beneath the sea of feet. Already many were underfoot, heads buried in their arms, sides, ribs and thighs bruised where they were kicked or trodden on. If it continued there would be disaster—greater disaster, for already there was tragedy enough. Many people were still in the chine, under that pile of earth which moved so sluggishly.

Loftus, at first afraid that he had started too late, thought that the pressure began easing slightly. A woman, crouching almost double, had her head in his stomach, pressing remorselessly, jammed against him by a big lout behind her. The man was one of the worst of the crowd, bellowing high-pitched cries of fear, and struggling wildly. Loftus tightened his grip on Carr's hand, leaned towards him and said:

'Try and hold it for a moment.'

Carr nodded.

Loftus released the policeman, bunched his fingers and leaned forward. His fist cracked against the lout's jaw. The man collapsed, helpless, on the shoulders of the others. Loftus felt the pressure increase for a moment, and could not find Carr's hand again; then he realized that someone had sprung forward and filled the gap.

In another five minutes the worst was over. Loftus and the

others backed away more quickly, people were moving more steadily, and the crowd began to thin out. Soon Carr's police took complete control. Many of them had been struggling in the middle of the stampede, to slow it down, and now that the panic had passed its height they were able to work more effectively.

But there was much to be done.

As the crowd thinned out little parties of people remained in the roadway. A child was crying in shrill, high-pitched screams, standing over the huddled figure of a woman, its mother, who lay quite still. A man joined them, and started to cry:

'Jennie, Jennie, Jennie!'

There were a dozen such scenes, and more than one mother was bending over the figure of her child, nearly hysterical with fear. All this Loftus saw in that garish, unholy light. His heart was heavy within him, for he had started this thing, the responsibility for every man, woman and child who was hurt rested on him.

He picked up the child, to try to stop its screams, but they grew worse. Fists in eyes, mouth wide open; there were moments when the little chap was silent as he drew in his breath to yell—and then the scream came, piercing and harrowing.

Someone pushed against Loftus.

'Give him to me,' said Polly, and she took the child.

Loftus gave her a quick grin, and then moved away.

Carr came out of the crowd and joined him.

'Doctors,' said Loftus.

'Some are here, some are being sent for,' said Carr. 'I sent word to the hospital and ordered a general call.'

'Good! Also rescue squads?'

'Yes,' said Carr. His fair face looked ghastly, and there was a scratch, bleeding freely, which ran from his eye to his mouth—where an hysterical woman had clawed at him. 'I hate to think of that bank.'

'So do I,' said Loftus. 'Let's get there.'

He looked round. George and Hoffmann and others of the Department were peering into the chine. They could see the path running through it, on which many people were hurrying to and fro. It was odd, but every face was clearly visible: if one of Rutter's men passed, he would be seen.

Loftus bellowed again.

'Keep watching!'

George and the others waved. Polly, sitting at the side of the road, was bouncing the child up and down; Loftus became aware that the screams had stopped. The man who had cried 'Jennie' was now on his knees, and his wife was sitting up dazedly. Others who had been prostrate were sitting up, also, but a few remained unmoving. Men were bending over them—the doctors. Two or three women in nurses' uniform were busy. A fluffy-haired, middle-aged woman in a dressing-gown and slippers was coming from the gate-way of a house, carrying a large tray on which was a tea-pot and a dozen cups. She stopped near Loftus.

'Bless you!' he said, and smiled at her. She laughed. 'Trust the people,' Loftus mused, 'after the first shock.'

There was some order, now. Many who had been among the first to scramble for safety were helping those who had been hurt. There was little confusion; the lights were invaluable, and there was no fumbling, no fear of chaos.

Loftus reached the edge of the bank where the landslide had started.

On the bank men and women were at the work of rescue. Many of them were knee-deep in sandy soil, some were clinging with one hand to the branches of trees and with the other to people who had been buried. It was an appalling sight. Loftus could have counted at least fifty heads above the earth—and here and there an arm, a foot, moving slightly. A man had been crushed by a tree. His eyes were wide open and his mouth shut tightly. A lad, no more than twelve, was pulling ineffectually at the tree.

Farther down, the path was completely covered by the soil. How deep was it? Loftus wondered.

'This way,' said Carr. 'You can't get down here.'

'No,' said Loftus, and hated his leg.

He passed some of his men. Hammond, with the help of several others, was working at a tree which pinned two people down. Here, where the fall had started, the people had received the worst shock. There was danger, too, of another fall.

Loftus walked along a stretch of road which was in shadows. There the lamps had been brought down in the landslide, and there was an eerie half-light. He walked, with Carr, past tall trees which now looked dark and sinister, until he came into the full light again. A stream of people walked in front of him. They reached the edge of the cliff, and then went down a narrow path. Loftus found it heavy going, but he reached the foot at last, and came to the beach, which was thronged with people.

Softly, soothingly, the sea murmured on the beach.

He walked towards the chine.

Parties passed him. Many people had already been rescued, and some were being carried, others helped along. Two ambulances drew up—they had come along the promenade—and from them sprang nurses of both sexes. A car from which three men appeared pulled up near Loftus.

'Doctors,' said Carr.

A lorry arrived, and a party of men jumped from it, carrying ropes, pick-axes, shovels.

'What organization!' exclaimed Loftus.

'Civil Defence,' said Carr.

The fallen soil on the path was thick in places, thin in others. Small trees, shrubs and branches lay across their path, but were already being moved to one side. Loftus got to the centre of the disturbance, and looked up. Ropes were dangling over the side of the chine, tied to trees or held by several men, and people extricated from the earth were laboriously making their way up. Some of the hands and legs were now freed of earth, and their owners were being dug out. In the space of half an hour a miracle had come about, but Loftus's heart was still heavy within him.

'Well,' said Carr, 'it's properly in hand.'

'Yes,' said Loftus. 'A masterly job.'

'But your people probably got away.'

'I wouldn't be surprised,' said Loftus. 'I haven't seen one of the beggars.'

'This *would* happen,' Carr said. 'I'd no idea the bank was unsafe.'

'Unsafe?' echoed Loftus, staring at him.

'Why, yes,' said Carr, puzzled. 'That's obvious.'

'My dear chap!' protested Loftus. 'Anything would be unsafe when high explosive goes off inside it.'

'*What?*'

'I thought you heard it,' Loftus said. 'There was the distinct roar of an explosion. This was no accident. There's nothing the matter with the chine, it stood the test miraculously, I expected far worse. Our Mr. Rutter is responsible for this.'

Carr seemed bereft of words.

Loftus meant what he said except in one small detail. That an explosion beneath the earth had started the landslide he had no doubt at all, but—*was* Rutter responsible? Indirectly he was, undoubtedly, but in Loftus's mind there was a thought which worried him more than anything else: T.N.25.

Dr. Morritz had been kidnapped in Paris, and might have been brought to England. Bournemouth was undoubtedly the centre of Rutter's activities, and it was not unlikely that somewhere here there had been work on T.N.25. If there had been an experimental laboratory, *under the earth*, much would be explained. If the reports he had received from Craigie were reliable, a thimbleful of T.N.25 could do this—and worse than this.

Hammond appeared unexpectedly. There was a crooked smile on his lips as he joined Loftus.

'Well?' he said.

'The worst hasn't happened,' said Loftus. 'Have you seen anyone?'

Hammond did not need to ask whom he meant by 'anyone', and shook his head.

'But I've been thinking,' he said.

'Yes,' said Loftus. 'It's a stimulus for thought. We were slow before. Go on.'

'The beggars didn't leave the chine by normal means because they didn't need to,' said Hammond. 'They went to earth. Probably they had tunnelled from one of the nearby houses and got through that way. The house would be fairly near the suspension bridge, I think.'

'Yes,' said Loftus. 'If they broke surface in a garden, our fellows couldn't have seen them. I'm beginning to think there are too many trees and thick hedges in Bournemouth!'

'You heard the explosion, didn't you?'

'Yes,' said Loftus. 'I've some ideas about that, too.'

'Experiment in T.N.25,' murmured Hammond.

'We ought to lecture on the mysteries of telepathy,' said

Loftus. 'Now we've reason to think that Rutter and his men disappeared into a house near here, and there's also reason to think that he was using that house as an experimental laboratory. Morritz was probably there all the time. The question is— did Rutter start the explosion for the sake of it, or did something just go wrong? If it went wrong—'

'Morritz and anyone with him went sky-high,' said Hammond.

'In any event, now we can dig in earnest, and find the tunnel, if there is one,' Loftus said. He turned to Carr, who had been talking to a uniformed police sergeant, and told him what he thought—without mentioning T.N.25. The possibility obviously worried Carr, but he raised no objections.

'As soon as we're sure all the people are out, we'll start digging for your tunnel,' he said. 'It will be morning before we can start, I'm afraid.'

'Can you pass the word round that the diggers might find one?' asked Loftus. 'Someone might strike it by accident.'

'Yes, I'll do that.'

'And then I want to know which of the houses fairly near the suspension bridge has recently changed hands,' said Loftus.

'Probably quite a number,' said Carr. 'Mildmay will probably be able to help you.'

'Who's Mildmay?'

'One of the biggest estate agents in the town, who handles a lot of property about here,' said Carr. 'He lives not ten minutes' walk away. Would you like to see him?'

'Very much,' said Loftus.

'I'll send a man with you,' said Carr. 'Sergeant...' He gave the sergeant instructions, which were passed on to a constable.

This man walked with Loftus, saying they would have to

go right to the top of the chine, because the nearest steps had been dislodged in the fall. They neared the suspension bridge where Loftus, looking up, stopped short. Several other people saw him look, and also glanced up.

Climbing from the branch of a tree which almost touched the bridge, was a man whose hand was stretched out to try to grip the bridge and who was swaying up and down. If he missed his grip, if he slipped once, he would crash down.

Loftus, his expression strained, recognized George Henry George.

12

MONKEY-TRICKS

One moment Polly had seen George by her side. She had handed over a smiling but tired child to its grateful parents, tactfully hinted that it should have been in bed hours earlier, and rejoined George at the vantage point. Then someone had attracted her attention, and she had looked round. The next moment, there was no George.

That alarmed her.

Then she saw him, half-way down the bank of the chine. Suddenly he leapt for the branch of a tree, swung from it and hauled himself up, swarmed along it, then dropped. Thus he got farther down, without having to go a long way round.

Her heart was in her mouth as she watched.

He moved with remarkable agility and speed. He tried the tree trick again, successfully, to avoid another detour.

Then she saw him drop to the ground.

She exclaimed aloud, for something in the way he dropped frightened her. Then he moved his head, and peered round a shrub. She saw that he had something in his right hand. She saw a faint light come from it, and fancied that she heard the report of a shot, but there was so much noise and so many cars were passing to and fro, that she could not be sure.

He got up cautiously, staring towards the end of the suspension bridge. She saw a man slip between the trees there.

He was bareheaded, and in the light his hair glinted red.

George had talked of a red-haired man.

Suddenly she saw the man again, this time swarming up a tree. He reached the underpart of the bridge, put his hands up and gripped it, and hauled himself up. It was done very quickly, and at a moment when George was unable to see him, because of the intervening branches. By the time George reached the same tree, the man was half-way over the rails of the bridge. From where she stood, Polly could see that he was being watched bewilderedly by half a dozen people on the bridge.

Then George appeared again. How he climbed the tree at such speed she did not know. Hardly a moment seemed to pass between the time he first appeared and the moment when he was standing on the tip of the swaying branch, one hand stretched out to grip the bridge.

She saw what Loftus, down below, could not see. The man with red hair had reached safety. The people on the bridge still seemed puzzled, and made no move when he took his hand from his pocket. She saw the gun in it, levelled towards George.

She screamed: 'George, look out, *look out!*'

George could not hear her, but he seemed to sense the danger. He swayed up and down, and two bullets missed him and were buried in the chine. Then he sprang upwards. For a moment he was suspended in mid-air, before he gripped the side of the bridge, and, with far greater agility than the red-haired man, reached the parapet and vaulted over.

The red-haired man turned and ran. The gun in his hand

scared most of the people on the bridge, but one jumped at him. Polly did not see a shot fired, but she saw the man who had made the attempt fall in his tracks. Two or three men were between George and his quarry, so George could not shoot. He bounded forward, sending men right and left.

The bridge thundered, echoing and re-echoing to the footsteps of the man with red hair, who was running desperately towards the east side of the chine. George went after him. People between them still prevented him from shooting.

Then, from the shrubs at the side of the path leading to the bridge, Hoffmann appeared. He simply put out his foot, and the red-haired man, taken unawares, fell over it. Hoffmann quickly followed up his advantage, and when George came up the red-haired man was half-conscious, for Hoffmann's fingers were pressing into the back of his neck, and the man could hardly breathe.

George, gulping for breath, muttered:

'Well, that's one of them, anyhow. Nice work, Hoffy.'

Hoffmann smiled, and the sadness was gone from his eyes for those few seconds.

While George, Hoffmann and Loftus, who had joined the party, were by the side of the road interrogating the red-haired man, who had the same remarkable loyalty to Rutter as Merryweather, and at first would not speak, Rutter, Lodge and two other men as well as Lodge's wife, were in a small room of a house overlooking Alum Chine.

Only Rutter seemed sure of himself; the others were unashamedly frightened.

'Red will return,' Rutter said, 'and if he should be detained, he will not talk. You are worried for no reason at all.'

Lodge muttered: 'Maurice isn't back, either.'

'Maurice has gone out on a special mission,' said Rutter. 'Keep quiet, Lodge. I have heard more than enough from you tonight.'

Lodge muttered: 'That's all very well—'

'We're mad to stay here,' gasped his wife, 'they'll find us, you know what Loftus is, they'll find us!'

'We are not leaving this house while the crowd is outside!' snapped Rutter. 'If I hear any more of this insolence, I'll deal with you in a way you won't forget. Go and stiffen your yellow hearts with whisky. Go on. Get out! But,' he added, as they moved towards the door, 'if one of you leaves the house without my permission, he will live *just* long enough to regret it.'

They went out, thoroughly cowed.

From a chair in the corner, where he was sitting with his hands tied to the arms, Bannister said:

'They aren't so brave, Rutter, are they?'

Rutter said: 'I told you to be quiet.' He hesitated for a moment, and then stepped towards his prisoner. He raised his right hand and struck Bannister across the face, and although Bannister saw the blow coming, he did not shift his position and he did not lose his smile.

'Did Loftus know this address?' Rutter demanded.

'If he didn't, he will soon find it out,' said Bannister, and added with a touch of impatience: 'Why waste your time on me, Rutter? If you're going to kill me, get it done. I won't give you information.'

'We will see,' said Rutter. He looked about to strike the big man again. His hand was raised for an appreciable time, and then he lowered it slowly and turned away.

The tunnel ran beneath the house, leading from the garden to the chine. Rutter knew that the rescue-workers might come across it, but it was useless at the moment to try to make his men work to save them from threatening disaster. Their nerve had gone. Red and Maurice, on whom he could most rely, had been away too long, Lodge was right about that.

Bannister knew that his own danger was greater than ever, for he now knew a great deal.

When he had first been brought to the house Bannister had been unconscious, but when he had come round he had heard Red and Lodge talking of the tunnel, and he knew how he had been brought out of the chine so easily. That was not surprising—and nor was it surprising that, when he had recovered sufficiently to walk, he had been led through the back garden, surrounded by trees and a thick laurel hedge— and overlooking the chine—to a small doorway of what looked like an air-raid shelter. He had gone down several steps, with Red in front of him and Rutter behind him, along a passage which smelt of damp earth.

He slipped from time to time, down more steps and along further stretches of the passage, until he came to another doorway.

The door was closed.

Rutter pressed a bell, and after a long time the door opened. It was of steel, electrically controlled. A bright light shone through, and as Bannister walked on he saw that beyond the door there was several feet of concrete. He had no idea that there was such a thing as T.N.25, but these precautions seemed to shout: *explosive.*

Little had been said to him.

There was a small room with concrete walls, another passage lined with concrete, and then he entered another brightly-lit room, larger than the first, with a bench along one side and all the equipment of a laboratory. By the bench stood a short, broad-shouldered man, clean-shaven, bald, with features which seemed bleached white and eyes that were like bright black coals.

'I have brought a friend of yours, Dr. Morritz,' said Rutter.

The man by the bench turned to look at them.

He started when he saw Bannister, and for a moment he stood quite still, with his arms raised. Then he took a step forward, and Bannister felt a genuine surge of hope. If Morritz accepted him, if he were sent to work with the Frenchman, there was no knowing what would result. Escape for both of them was not out of the question, there was even a chance of leading Loftus and the others to this point...

And then Morritz backed away.

He drew himself to his full height, and on his white face and in his burning eyes was a withering contempt which even Bannister felt.

'You do not deceive me,' said Morritz. His English was good, but he had a strong French accent.

'This is Professor Toller,' Rutter said, but he looked at Bannister with doubt in his eyes for the first time.

'You do not deceive me,' repeated Morritz.

'But, my dear friend—' Bannister stepped forward, his hands outstretched, imploring. 'I received your message, I have come to—'

'You have come to *pretend* that you are Toller,' said Morritz. 'You wish to obtain all the knowledge which I have of this great discovery. I will work here,' said Morritz, and his eyes seemed to burn, 'I will work until I have perfected everything, *everything*! And then, rather than allow it to be used by such men as you, I will destroy it. I will destroy this room and all the people in it! I will not allow this discovery to be used by such men!'

'But I agree with you,' said Bannister, desperately. 'I am in full agreement, my friend. Who—who *are* these men? They brought me a message. They said that they wished to bring us together again, and I—I was delighted. I did not know that you had no regard for them.'

Morritz cried: 'I am not a fool. I know my friends. I have worked with Toller for many years. *You* are not Professor Toller.'

Bannister said: 'I assure you—'

'Be quiet,' said Rutter. He stepped forward and looked into Morritz's eyes. 'You are sure about this man?'

'I am *quite* sure,' said Morritz. 'Look!' he cried, and he stepped forward and seized Bannister's hands. 'Are they the hands of an old man? Are they?'

He held up Bannister's right hand and raised his own alongside it. One had the veins thick, the skin wizened, the flesh mottled, the other, in spite of all the effort that Bannister had made, was by comparison too firm.

Morritz flung the hand aside, and turned back to the bench. Rutter struck Bannister a vicious blow, and Morritz turned, saw Bannister stumbling, and gasped in sudden horror:

'What have I done? What have I done?'

'I am very grateful to you, Doctor,' said Rutter, and with the red-haired man he took Bannister's arm and led him outside, leaving Morritz staring after them, distraught, despairing.

Bannister had expected to die.

There had been one slim chance from the beginning—that, if the truth about him were discovered, Rutter would look on him as a hostage, and perhaps as a source of information.

Rutter did just that.

Since then, the explosion had shaken the building and caused a panic among the occupants as great as on the cliffs. Lodge, his wife and the others had wanted to leave at once. Rutter had kept them there, for one good reason—he knew that all the police in Bournemouth, perhaps in all nearby counties, were on watch that night. The roads would probably be watched, he did not think there was any chance of getting away from Bournemouth.

There was one other house where he could find temporary refuge, near the chine—*but he did not know where it was.*

In Bannister's mind there was no doubt of what had happened. Morritz, driven to a point of utter desperation, had blown up the laboratory and himself with it. There was no hope for Morritz, but it was evident now that he had been working on an explosive.

Did Loftus know that? Bannister wondered.

He watched Rutter standing and smoking there, his face expressionless. George's words came to his mind, and Bannister could not repress a smile. 'Old Iron Face' was apt.

Rutter felt the time dragging, and felt as cold and tense as he looked. He had not been able to telephone 'Noel'; he had tried, but the explosion had destroyed the telephone cables. So Maurice had gone out to telephone from a kiosk, and he had been gone too long. Loftus's men had probably seen him. Red should be back, too.

A bell rang outside.

Rutter moved swiftly, went out of the room and slammed the door behind him. Bannister strained at his bonds, but could not make any impression on them. He heard voices. The door opened, and Maurice, excited, unscathed, finished by saying:

'He insisted—only you and I, only you and I.'

'We need the others,' said Rutter.

'They can take their chance,' said Maurice. 'Except that fine gentleman.' He looked malignantly at Bannister, but Rutter made no comment.

'We need the others,.' he repeated, 'and we shall need this man. I will go and see him.'

'He'll never give way,' said Maurice.

'He *must* give way,' said Rutter, and he went out again.

The front door slammed.

In the moment that it was open, Bannister heard the noises from outside, excited voices, cars passing swiftly, voices raised to clear a path for the cars. He had some idea of what must have happened, but could not guess the full extent of it. He looked at Maurice, who stared at him for a few moments; and he knew that thought of murder was passing through the man's mind.

Then Maurice went out.

Mr. Mildmay was remarkably like his name. He was small, affable, soft-voiced, with smiling eyes and a calm manner— the manner of a man who was always exerting himself to please all with whom he came in contact. Yes, there were several houses on the east side of Alum Chine which had changed hands recently.

'Let me see. *The Gables*, Pendleton's handled that, by auction, in July. That is within a few yards of the chine, just across the road from where the explosion occurred.'

'Explosion?' echoed Loftus.

'I am sure you heard it,' said Mildmay. 'In fact I have already telephoned the Editors of the local papers and told them that I *distinctly* heard it, and other people agree with me. Now let me see, *Blue Tiles*. We sold that to Colonel Broderick in June—or was it early July? June, I think. And *Mountebank*—a curious name for a house, isn't it?—we also sold that in April. *Chineside* is a smaller property, Wilson's sold that in April or May.' He made pencil notes on a map, and went on talking.

'Do you know which of these has been occupied for a few weeks or more?' asked Loftus.

'*Blue Tiles* and *The Gables* are still in the hands of the decorators,' said Mildmay. '*Mountebank* has not yet been touched. *Chineside*, now—there appeared to be a lot of repair work necessary on that house, workmen were busy for some weeks. And curiously enough, *not* employed by a local contractor. It puzzled me.' He blinked at Loftus. '*Chineside* was occupied in early June, Mr. Loftus. There are others, of course, but if you look at the map'—his pencil touched a red patch with a blue line, and then moved across the map—'you will see that *Chineside* is a little south of the bridge, at a point where the chine is steepest. Are you looking for tunnels, Mr. Loftus?'

Loftus smiled. 'You're very shrewd.'

'How nice of you to say so,' chirruped Mr. Mildmay. 'I like to *try* to use my mind. *Chineside*, we are interested then in that house. Can I help you further, I wonder? I take a regular walk on West Overcliff Drive, and often pass the house. I have noticed two or three people enter it. *Can* I help, I wonder?'

'What were they like to look at?' asked Loftus.

'There was a remarkably *handsome* man. Rather flashily-dressed, I thought, but quite remarkably handsome. And a very big man with red hair. I noticed him, because he was the foreman of the workmen who did the repairs, and I thought it strange that he should be a frequent visitor after the repairs were finished. I wonder—'

'Mr. Mildmay,' said Loftus, with feeling, 'you're little short of manna from heaven! *Chineside* it is. You'll excuse me, won't you?'

'My dear sir, of course! And you are very kind!'

Loftus beamed on him, and went out. Within half an hour, a cordon of police and Department Z men were closing in on *Chineside*.

13

'CHINESIDE'

A ll ready?' asked Loftus.

'All set,' said Hammond.

'Then we won't waste time,' said Loftus. 'Come on, George, stop squeezing Polly's arm.'

'I resent that,' said George, leaving Polly's side promptly. 'I was urging her to go home. She's looking tired out.'

'It's a good idea,' said Loftus, but he made no effort to persuade Polly. She watched the three men open the gate of the house called *Chineside* and walk up the long, winding path.

Some men were in the grounds, some in the street outside, some in the grounds of the neighbouring houses. It would be virtually impossible for anyone to escape—if, thought Loftus, who felt a little blue, anyone was now within.

'Bell, knocker or just forced entry?' asked George.

'Bell and knocker,' said Loftus.

'Okay,' said George, and pressed the bell while Hammond banged on the door. 'We shall probably scare 'em into making a run for it, and they won't choose the front door, so we shall miss the fun.'

There was no answer.

'Let me show you what a wizard I am with locks,' pleaded George. 'I'll have that open in half a jiff.' He peered forward. The light from the flood-lamps was still bright, and when he stood on one side he could see clearly. He frowned. 'But can I? A pretty nifty lock, that, and the door's all wood. No glass to break.' He tapped it. 'Pretty solid, too. Windows?'

'Go and look,' said Loftus.

George disappeared from the porch. There was still no sound from inside the house, and when George returned, after a few minutes, he had an owlish expression.

'Shutters,' he said. 'Steel, thick, locked. We could do with a spot of high ex., Bill.'

Then came a shout from the rear of the house.

George was on the porch one moment and on the drive the next. Loftus and Hammond exchanged grins, but did not move. If there were a sortie from the back, it might be a feint. The front door might be used for the main sortie because it seemed the most unlikely place. They heard nothing from inside the house, but there were scuffling noises at the back— and then, sharp and clear, the report of a shot.

At the back, a door was open.

There was no light from inside the house, but the glow from the flood-lighting showed George Henry George the open door and the men who were rushing from the house. The waiting police pounced on them. One man—a little fellow whom George recognized as Pimple Face, and who had nearly got free—used a gun. He missed the man at whom he fired, and was soon flat on his back.

George reached the open door a yard ahead of Mike and Mark Errol. Powerful torches shone into the scullery and then the kitchen, but the house was silent and they met no one.

Other men came in.

'Room by room,' said Mike Errol, 'and don't take chances, George, we want you to amuse us another day.'

'Thank you kindly, sir,' said George.

He took no chances; he frequently amazed the Errols as well as others by his competence. He turned the handle of a door, stepped to one side, and then flung the door open. Crouching, he went in swiftly, with a gun in his hand, moving so fast that it was doubtful whether a chance shot would hit him. He did that three times, and then he darted into a room where the light was on.

'Careful!' cried Mike.

George went in as if worked by a spring. They saw him disappear, saw his shadow—and then saw him straighten up.

He said: 'All clear,' but there was a subdued note in his voice. The Errols followed him, while other men went upstairs to complete the search.

Tied to a chair, his head lolling forward, was Bannister.

All of them thought he was dead, he was so motionless and in such an odd position. George stepped to his side and, very gently, raised his head. Bannister's eyes were closed. George felt his pulse. In a flash there was a new light in his eyes and a vast grin on his face.

'He's ticking!' he cried. 'It's a bump on the head, they didn't kill him!'

They had not killed Bannister, said little, frightened Lodge, soon afterwards, because they had been afraid of capture and did not want murder on their hands. True, he had fired at a man in the grounds, but he had lost his head, he had not meant murder. His pimply face was a pasty grey, and he was trembling as Loftus, Carr and Hammond stood in front of him in one of the rooms at *Chineside*. His wife was with him, wringing her hands, and Maurice stood in a corner with two other prisoners—a silent Maurice who hid his fear well.

Lodge babbled on.

They knew that 'the Old Doc' was working on some high explosive, that was all. They had taken great precautions to make sure that there was no serious effect if the stuff went off. 'The Old Doc' had stayed in the laboratory; he, Lodge, had disliked going into the work-room, although he had sometimes taken the old man's meals in. All of them knew that 'the Old Doc' had threatened to blow them all to hell, but had not taken his threat seriously. Yes, 'the Old Doc' had come from Paris, Maurice had brought him over.

Maurice turned his malignant gaze on the little man.

'He did!' cried Lodge. 'I know it was Maurice! If he'd had *his* way, he would have killed your pal, he would really; if it hadn't been for me he would have been killed—and *we* would have been hanged,' added Lodge, desperately. 'I'll do some things, but not murder—no, not me.'

'All right,' said Loftus. 'Where did Rutter go?'

'I dunno,' cried Lodge, 'I swear I dunno. There's a man he knows, staying somewhere in Bournemouth, he went to see him, the rat! He knew we'd be for it, he got out. Unless'— Lodge looked suddenly hopeful— 'unless *you* got him, mister.'

Loftus said: 'We didn't.'

'And you won't,' said Maurice.

Gordon Craigie smiled across the fireplace at Loftus, who was sitting in an easy chair. It was the following morning, and Loftus had travelled up from Bournemouth after a short night's rest. He did not show any effect of his exertions, however, and had told the story simply and graphically.

Sitting on the arm of a chair, staring at him, was the Rt. Hon. Herbert Mattley, the Prime Minister. A thin, thoughtful-looking man with a pale face, shrewd eyes and a rather wide mouth, he had smoked cigarette after cigarette and had not once interrupted Loftus's narrative. Nor had he moved—like Leven, he had the trick of keeping still.

Loftus looked at him.

'That's as far as we've got, sir. I think it's as well that Rutter got away. If we had caught him, I feel sure that he would not have talked, and we would have no one to look for.'

Mattley, surprisingly, smiled.

'And that wouldn't do at all!'

'You agree that Rutter isn't the principal in this business, I hope?' said Loftus.

'Fully,' said Mattley. He took the cigarette out of his mouth and looked at the long piece of grey ash. 'Yes, I fully agree. And you've done well again, Loftus, you people always do well. I'm told you think it's a matter of private interests, Craigie.'

'I do,' said Craigie.

Mattley put the cigarette back, and scowled.

'I wish I could be sure. I'm not. Still, you don't often guess wrong.' He was quiet for a moment, and then he stood up and walked to the far end of the room. He turned his back to Craigie's desk, leaned against it, and said deliberately:

'I came back early, Craigie, because I have received further information.'

'Yes?' said Craigie, but he felt the effect of Mattley's words and the careful manner in which they were uttered. Something unpleasant was coming, a thing which had brought the Prime Minister back from Paris three days before he was due.

Loftus sat quite still.

Mattley said slowly: 'In both Washington and Moscow approaches have been made to high Government officials. Information has been lodged that we and the French together are preparing a new high explosive. The formula has been offered to both Moscow and Washington—at a price.'

Loftus said quickly: 'It may be a fake.'

'Yes,' said Mattley. 'Yes, it may be a false formula, but we can't be sure. The repercussions might be serious. In fact they are already serious. A full statement is being sent to both Washington and Moscow. We must convince them of our goodwill. That's hardly your job,' he added, with a quick, understanding smile, 'but we now want to know *who* offered them the formula, whether it's a genuine one or not.'

Craigie said: 'Doesn't the offer support my contention— that there's a commercial interest behind it?'

'Not necessarily,' said Mattley. 'There is another possibility. It may be so obvious that you have missed it, but it has given me great anxiety. There have been suggestions in isolationist American newspapers and magazines, as well as thinly veiled accusations in most countries, that Great Britain and the Commonwealth are returning to power politics.' A wintry smile crossed the Prime Minister's face. 'Whatever they may be!' he interjected, and Loftus and Craigie smiled. 'Leaving a definition of the term to others,' continued Mattley, 'we have to admit that if it were seriously considered likely by the United States, Soviet Russia and by other countries, that we are endeavouring to establish spheres of influence, other than the influence we already exert on behalf of the United Nations, great and perhaps irremediable harm would be done.

'It would not be difficult for certain elements to make great capital out of this, since we have allowed the experiments to proceed and, in fact, have given Toller every facility for his work.' He paused, looking straight at Loftus, and again he smiled unexpectedly. 'Now, Loftus, harbour no evil thoughts! What are you thinking?'

Loftus said: 'It would have saved a lot of trouble if we had told both Moscow and Washington when we first started.'

'Yes,' said Mattley. 'It is no answer to say: such information was sent but did not arrive. No answer,' he added, as Loftus started and even Craigie stirred in his chair, 'that will satisfy, or pacify, the hunger of those who have nothing but bad to say for our administration. However, it is true.'

'Diplomatic bags rifled?' asked Loftus. Even he found it difficult to keep out of his voice a note of surprise, which might have been taken for scepticism.

'Even worse,' said Mattley. 'Confidential statements were sent to the respective Embassies in London. Acknowledgments of the statements were made and we were told that the documents had been sent to the respective capitals. Some documents were. They covered an innocuous experiment which is being made relative to jet-propulsion. The original documents were replaced by these unimportant papers *before* they left Whitehall. There is a job for you, Craigie!'

'How long ago?' asked Loftus, sharply.

'Seven weeks.'

'What has caused the delay in finding out?'

'There was no reason why we should expect a detailed reply, no reason why Washington or Moscow should send one. Not until I realized that something was amiss did I make inquiries. I have today received cables which make the situation clear. Some highly-placed and trusted person has betrayed us, so whether there is a formula in existence or is not, much harm has already been done. I have reason to believe that a detailed account of the experiments and an open accusation that we have deliberately deceived our friends will appear in the American Press. It will doubtless be taken up by ours. If at this juncture in the affairs of mankind,' continued Mattley, very softly, 'there should be an open rift, on any score whatsoever, between Moscow, Washington and London, incalculable harm will be done. I have already said that it might be irremediable.' He paused, looked at his cigarette again, and said:

'Find who is behind this, Craigie, at all costs. There is too much at stake for us to take a single chance. Let your men know the truth, and give them my views on it. Find me the man who betrayed us in Whitehall, and find everything relevant—*soon!*'

Craigie pressed the button in the mantelpiece.

Mattley nodded, gave his wintry smile, and went out as the door opened. The shadowy figures of his Special Branch police guards appeared on the cold stone steps.

'Well, well,' said Loftus. 'Pop up and get me the moon, Gordon, I'll take the hard job.'

14

THE HARD JOB

I t was in the nature of things that the task which threatened the Department as an impasse should be easily accomplished, and that which looked easy and straightforward should be most difficult. Keeping track of Rutter in Bournemouth had seemed easy; yet three days after Mattley had talked to Craigie and Loftus, the Department men in the South Coast town were beginning to believe that Rutter had escaped from them. Those agents who were summoned to London, however, including Bannister, who had not been badly hurt, and the Errols, had what appeared to be the most difficult task—to find who had tampered with the documents sent to Washington and Moscow.

On the third day, Mike and Mark Errol pressed the button beneath the hand-rail outside Craigie's office, and when, after due formality, they entered the room, Mike was smiling and there was a gleam of satisfaction in his cousin's eyes.

Craigie was there alone.

'The documents were prepared at the Offices of the Cabinet,' said Mark, while Mike lit a cigarette and showed that for once he was leaving all the talking to his cousin, 'and there were five people who had access to them—all highly placed. The documents were not seen by any member of the clerical staff, they were typed by one of the five, checked by the others, prepared jointly. Mattley read the whole thing to the Cabinet, where it was fully discussed, so only a Cabinet Minister or one of the five men could have jockeyed with the thing. The Cabinet Ministers are out—'

'Pity,' murmured Mike, 'No sensation.'

'The high officials, one by one, came before our ken,' said Mark, 'and we had them all carefully watched, as per instruction.' Obviously he was enjoying this revelation, and Craigie did nothing to spoil his pleasure. 'One Bentley, Hubert Wilberforce Bentley, O.B.E., who is a forty-ish gentleman of expensive habits and for some time has lost much money at the gaming-tables—'

'A fact on which his girl friend enlightened us,' said Mike. 'And what a girl friend! Sleek, svelte, mink and sable, brittle like glass, beautiful like picture post-cards. Sorry, Mark, Go on.'

'At the gaming-tables, which no respectable man should frequent,' said Mark, 'and being responsible for many bills run up by the girl friend—we are being polite, you understand—and having a useful but not remarkable salary and, as far as we could ascertain, no large private income—'

'How did you get that?' asked Craigie.

Mark smiled. 'We put Miller on to it.'

Superintendent Miller, of New Scotland Yard, was the liaison officer between the Yard and the Department, and was rarely slow in getting results for which its agents asked.

'Where was I?' asked Mark.

'You've got one more sentence,' said Mike, warningly. 'The bit about him taking a day off yesterday.'

'Oh yes,' said Mark. 'Hubert Wilberforce Bentley did not appear at the office yesterday, and remained—it was thought— at his flat. However, in the early afternoon he left the flat and, with a harassed, hunted look—'

'Oi!' interrupted Mike.

'Sorry, your turn,' said Mark, gracefully.

'Thank you. We split the story into two parts and drew lots who should have the climax,' explained Mike, and Craigie chuckled in spite of his tense interest. 'As Mark was saying, Bentley had a hang-dog-is-there-any-one-following-me-look about him. We were. He didn't see us. He went to Waterloo and I'll give you one guess where he booked for—'

'Bournemouth,' said Craigie, automatically.

'Bournemouth *West*,' improved Mike. 'The nearest station to Alum Chine. So we also booked, and I sent Loftus a wire and told him to have the station watched, in case our Hubert cottoned on to us and we wanted to complete his discomfiture. A very serious man, Bentley. He sat in his first-class carriage and looked grimly into space all the time. At Bournemouth West he hurried out, got a taxi, and George Henry George was waiting at the station in another. Off we went.' Mike paused, and beamed his broadest. 'Bentley drove straight to *Chineside*!'

'Not bad!' said Mark.

'He would have been seen and reported whether we'd been after him or not,' said Mike. 'However, he walked up the drive and rang the bell, and you should have seen his face when Bannister opened the door. Bannister as he is, not the Professor. There was much ado and many apologies, and Bentley came back with his tail between his legs. So, we've got him.'

'Orders, please,' said Mark.

'Where is he now?' asked Craigie.

'At his flat, communing with himself,' said Mike. 'Hammond and Dunster came back with us, and they're watching the place. A woman is there—perhaps the girl friend. On the whole—'

'Not at all bad,' said Craigie, smiling, 'There's only one thing missing.'

'Don't say it,' said Mike.

'It leads only to Rutter,' said Mark.

When they had gone, Craigie went to his desk and lifted a telephone. It was a direct line to 10, Downing Street. He gave his name to the first secretary who answered, and in a few moments Mattley was on the line.

'Yes, Craigie?'

'We have got as far as finding the man who substituted the documents,' said Craigie. 'A man named Bentley—' He paused, to give the Prime Minister an opportunity to comment, but Mattley did not take it. 'Hammond and the Errols have gone to his flat, with instructions to get a written confession,' said Craigie, 'and judging from the reports, he is in a pretty nervous state and shouldn't be too difficult.'

'Hu Bentley,' said Mattley, and there was an unusual note in his voice. 'I'm sorry about that. All right, Craigie. I am very glad you've got results so quickly. Have you anything else yet?'

'Not yet,' said Craigie.

'Try not to lose a minute,' said Mattley.

From that brief remark, Craigie judged that the situation was no easier than it had been. He had waited daily for an outburst in the American Press, or a caustic article in *Red Star* or *Pravda*, but so far the story had not broken. If the whole truth could be discovered before it did, much misunderstanding would be avoided, much bitterness left unstirred.

He worked at the desk, studying various reports about the activities of five armament manufacturers—but for once his mind was not on his task.

Bruce Hammond did not believe in taking chances.

He took Mark Errol with him up to Bentley's flat. Mike was outside at the front, with another agent, Dunster and yet a fourth were at the back. Bentley could not escape, and, to set the seal on the preparations, there were Special Branch policemen at either end of the street and the service alley behind it.

The street was a narrow turning between Piccadilly and Regent Street. There were a few inexpensive shops, next door to expensive *salons*, but most of the houses were grey, tall and narrow, unconnected with any kind of commerce.

Hammond rang the bell.

There was no immediate answer, but before he rang again footsteps sounded and the door was opened by a trim little maid, a middle-aged woman with a quick, attractive smile.

'We would like to see Mr. Bentley,' said Hammond.

'I'm sorry, sir,' she said, 'but Mr. Bentley is unwell, he is not able to see anyone.'

Hammond took out his card, showed it to her, and stepped past her while she looked at it in dismay. Mark sent her a reassuring smile, but did not relieve her anxiety. She followed them as they walked into the large, roomy hall.

Four doors led from the hall.

'Which is Mr. Bentley's bedroom?' asked Hammond.

'*Really*, sir, Mr. Bentley is too ill even to see the police. He mustn't be disturbed, he gave *strict* instructions.'

She came out with 'police' before either of the others could stop her, and her protestations were so loud that anyone in the flat must surely have heard her. Then a door opened, and a woman stepped through.

Her hair was a glossy black, dressed most attractively in Victorian style. Her face was a pale cream, with little colour. She had on a touch of lip-stick, but wore no rouge. Perhaps her pallor made her eyes seem so bright, and brought out the darkness of the lashes and eyebrows.

'Good morning,' she said. 'May, did I hear you say that these gentlemen are from the police?'

'Well, they showed a *card* from the police,' said May. She looked indignant, and added: 'I've told them they can't see Mr. Hubert, Miss Paula.'

Hammond said: 'I'm afraid we must.'

'Miss Paula' returned his steady gaze, and he did not think that she was puzzled. She was in the late twenties, he judged, but in some ways she looked much older. There was a quiet confidence and a poise about her which attracted him and impressed Mark.

She was not surprised by the appearance of the police.

'May I know why?' she asked.

'I'm afraid not,' said Hammond.

She hesitated, and then said, 'Please come with me. All right, May,' she added in an aside, and the little maid, with a backward glance, walked slowly towards another door.

Hammond thought: 'I must be careful, she's too disarming', and a similar thought was in Mark's mind.

'Miss Paula' led the way to a third door, which was closed. She hesitated for a moment, then turned her dark eyes on them and said quietly: 'Please don't make a noise.' She opened the door and stood aside for them to enter. Hammond went in cautiously, and Mark stood on the threshold, motioning to the woman. She followed Hammond.

Hubert Wilberforce Bentley was in bed, either asleep or unconscious. He was remarkably like 'Miss Paula', and there was little doubt that they were brother and sister. Bentley did not seem to be breathing. His dark hair was brushed straight back from his high, pale forehead and his lips were set tightly, as if he had been in pain. The room was tidy, the bedclothes almost symmetrical.

Hammond murmured: 'How long has he been like this?'

'For an hour,' said the woman. 'I hope you won't disturb him.'

'It would take a lot to do that,' said Hammond. He took Bentley's left hand, which lay on the turned-down sheet, and felt the pulse. It was very slow. He put a hand to Bentley's face. The woman made an involuntary movement to stop him, but changed her mind.

Bentley's eyes looked dull, and the pupils were dilated. He did not stir, and Hammond let the eyelid fall back again; it did so slowly, in an uncanny way.

'Have you called a doctor?' asked Hammond.

'No,' she said.

She had not wanted them to prove that he had been drugged, but the fact that he was drugged did not come to her as a surprise. She knew or guessed a great deal.

'My brother will recover without a doctor,' said 'Miss Paula'. 'I cannot grant you the right to interfere.'

'I see,' said Hammond. 'Shall we go into another room?'

She led the way, and waited by the door, closing it gently. The flat was very quiet, and their footsteps on the thin-pile carpet made only a faint sound. She opened the door of another room, large, bright, cool.

'Please sit down,' said Paula. 'As you will have gathered, I am Paula Bentley—Hubert's sister. May I ask you to explain your visit? And may I ask your names?'

Hammond said: 'I am Hammond, this is Mr. Mark Errol.' He showed his card, a card like that which had once so startled Polly, with the grey Z and the rest of the matter superimposed. She looked at it for some seconds, and then handed it back. She did not appear greatly surprised by his authority.

'Thank you. Can I be of any help?' she asked.

'I don't know,' said Hammond. 'Miss Bentley, I must tell you this. Mr. Bentley is, I believe, in possession of information of great importance. It is essential that he should confirm or deny certain facts for us, as soon as he comes round from his drugged sleep. I shall have to wait here until then, and I shall have to summon a doctor to see whether it is possible to bring your brother round before he would normally come round—*and*,' he added, grimly, 'to make sure that he is not seriously ill.'

'He is not', she said. 'He took a dose of laudanum. It is not for the first time.' There was no challenge in her eyes, and she did not question the 'drugged' sleep at all. 'He will probably sleep until this evening—won't that be time enough?'

'No,' said Hammond.

'What do you think he knows?'

'I am not at liberty to discuss it with you,' said Hammond. 'On the other hand, if you know why he has been so distracted recently, why he went to Bournemouth yesterday, and why he saw fit to drug himself, you must tell me.'

She kept still for some time, and then, to their surprise, she rose abruptly from her chair. Her hands clenched, and colour flooded her cheeks.

'That *damned* woman!' she said, and when she looked at them there was great pain in her eyes, 'What has he done?'

'Don't you know?' countered Hammond.

'Has he—betrayed—' She broke off, and turned to look out of the window. The emotion which she had kept back so determinedly was coming to the fore, and she was trembling. 'Has he sold state secrets?' she demanded, in a voice which was only just audible.

'Probaby,' said Hammond. 'He's certainly tried to.'

Mark, sitting near the door, looked at the woman with a sympathy which he could not keep out of his expression, but Hammond's face showed no sign of his feelings. He was a brown man, she was a black-and-white woman; they seemed to fit naturally into those colours.

She turned round again.

'I was afraid of that. He telephoned me this morning, asked me to come and see him. He told me that he had made a fool of himself, and that he was afraid of the consequences. He was— short of money. He has spent a great deal lately, one way and another. I did not press him to give me details of his difficulty, but nothing that he has done would surprise me. He was not— himself—when that woman—'

'What woman?' asked Hammond.

'A friend of his. Miss Gertrude Ryall.'

Hammond looked at Mark, who nodded; Gertrude Ryall was the 'girl friend' who had dispensed the information, and whatever Paula thought of her was probably near the mark.

'He was in love with her,' she said. The words seemed wrung from her. 'Her influence over him was malign. There was nothing he would not do at her request, and now—he has ruined himself and sold his country.' The phrase, uttered in a low-pitched, agonized voice, did not seem stilted. As if to herself, she went on: 'For three centuries a Bentley has—'

She broke off, and her eyes were very bright.

Hammond said: 'I am sorry that I have to question you, Miss Bentley, but there is no way in which I can avoid it, and the matter is urgent. May Mr. Errol use your telephone?'

'Of course.'

'Ask Dr. Little to come, Mark, will you?' asked Hammond, and then turned towards the girl as Mark went to a telephone which was in the corner of the room.

She made no protest, and Hammond went on:

'About Miss Ryall. Did you infer that she deliberately asked your brother to tamper with documents relating to his work?'

'Of course I did,' she said. 'That is why she encouraged him.'

'Then he hasn't known her for long?'

'For three months,' she said, 'and from the day he met her he has been a different man, he—' She broke off, and bit her lips. 'I am sorry. Please go on.'

'Have you any reason to believe that she persuaded him to interfere with these documents?'

'Yes. Before he went to sleep he said that she had asked him to do it. He was completely disillusioned, and in great distress. He did not mention documents, nor say what he had done, but I had no doubt that it was serious.'

'I see,' said Hammond. 'Do you know Miss Ryall well?'

'No. I met her only through my brother.'

'Is she well known among his circle of acquaintances?'

'I do not think so. I do not know where she came from. I believe that he met her when he was in Birmingham, on official business.'

'Birmingham,' murmured Mark. He had finished at the telephone, and turned and looked at Hammond. Kelly, the man who had taken Bannister's place as the Professor, had left a house in Birmingham. 'Do you know her Birmingham address?' Mark asked.

'No,' said Paula.

'Telephone Gordon,' said Hammond to Mark.

'Not before it's time,' said Mark. 'What the dickens were

Mike and I playing at?' He looked angry with himself, for he had taken it for granted that Gertrude Ryall had no interest in Bentley except the good time she could get out of him. Later, when he had pondered on it, Mike acknowledged that it was because he lacked that little something which Hammond, Loftus and Craigie possessed.

He heard Craigie speak and announced himself in the usual way. When he had half-finished his story about Gertrude Ryall, Craigie interrupted with a laugh.

'All right, Mark, there's no need to worry about it. I started inquiries about her as soon as she was mentioned.'

'Oh,' said Mark. 'Oh yes, you would. Good!'

'How are you getting on there?'

'You'd better have a word with Bruce,' said Mark.

When Hammond replaced the receiver, he advanced towards Paula, smiling but giving the impression that his was a distasteful task.

'When the doctor has made the examination,' he said, 'it will be necessary to take your brother to a nursing home, where he can be under constant surveillance. That is not because we would not trust him here with you, but because he might be in some danger.'

'Danger,' said Paula. 'Yes, of course.'

The front-door bell rang.

'That will be Doc Little,' said Mark. 'I'll go.'

He went out, waved the maid back as she appeared from the kitchen, and went to the door. Dr. Little, who lived near by, was the Department's doctor. He was frequently called in on such tasks as this and he had long since given up his practice so as to be available at any time. He was a very large, very fat man, another Loftus in appearance, and a jovial fellow to boot. Mark even prepared his lips for a smile of greeting.

A dark, slim stranger stood on the threshold.

'Er—good morning,' said Mark, nonplussed.

'Good morning,' said the stranger, touching his thin dark moustache. 'Mr. Bentley is expecting me, I think.'

'Is he?' said Mark. 'I—'

And then the stranger drove his clenched fist into Mark's stomach, and darted into the hall.

15

PAULA BENTLEY

Hammond heard the thud which followed Mark's gasp. He swung round and reached the door in a few strides, pulled it open—and stared into the hall. Mark was on the floor, trying to get up and to press his hands against his stomach at the same time. The maid was staring, open-mouthed, petrified with horror.

The bedroom door was open.

Hammond reached the room and went inside—and as he did so there was a single shot. Hammond stood helpless as a hole appeared in Bentley's forehead. He pushed the door back, believing that the assailant was hiding behind it, but the door hit the wall and swung back. The stranger, who had been hiding behind the wardrobe, leapt out and tried to slam the door in Hammond's face. It struck Hammond's foot and went back. The stranger was revealed for a moment, gun in hand. He ran at Hammond, who stretched out an arm to stop him.

The man fired point-blank.

The maid screamed.

Paula Bentley saw Hammond stagger, saw Mark still trying

to get up, his face distorted with pain, and saw the dark man with the gun. He caught sight of her as he made for the open front door, and waved the gun wildly. The maid began to scream at the top of her voice, high-pitched, ear-splitting screams.

On the hall table was a gong on a brass stand. Paula picked the hammer up by the handle attached to the round, leather head, and as the man with the gun backed away, she flung it at him. He was taken by surprise, and dodged to one side. Paula ran at him, while the maid's screams grew louder. There was bedlam in and below the flat, for voices sounded downstairs and doors banged.

The hammer hit the wall and bounced back against the man with the gun, proving enough to spoil his aim. Paula reached him and caught his wrist. He tried to wrench himself free, but failed. He drew back his free hand and drove it towards her stomach—but as he did so, Mike Errol appeared on the landing, and struck the man on the back of the head.

The murderer's fist scraped past Paula's waist. She held on to the man's wrist until Mike relieved her.

Mike twisted; the gun dropped.

'Pick it up, will you?' Mike asked Paula, calmly.

The girl obeyed, and stood for a moment with the automatic in her hand, breathing heavily. Then she looked at Hammond, who had not stirred. Other men appeared in the flat, most of them strangers to her, but there were one or two from flats in the same building.

She put the gun on the table and walked to Hammond. As she reached him, she glanced into the bedroom and saw her brother. There was a patch of red on his forehead, and blood had trickled down into his eyes.

Clearly he was dead.

She took a step towards him, stopped and turned round.

Then she went down on one knee by Hammond's side. He had been wounded in the chest, and the blood was spilling slowly to the carpet. Her hands were icy cold as she felt his pulse; it was beating.

He was unconscious, and there was an expression of dismay on his face.

A man said: 'Hallo, hallo, what's all this?'

Into the flat strode Dr. Little—'Doc' to the Department. By then Mark was leaning against the wall, trying to regain his breath, and Dunster was also in the bedroom.

Paula took May into the sitting-room, made her sit down, and poured out some whisky. She stood, soothing the little woman while the men took possession of the flat. Mark had recovered enough to play his part, although his stomach was still painful. The prisoner, who had not uttered a word since Mike had arrived and struck him, was standing in a corner. Two Special Branch men were watching him, but he was not hand-cuffed. Doc Little examined Hammond and found the wound a little too much to one side to be fatal, but Hammond was still unconscious.

An ambulance arrived, and Hammond was carried out on a stretcher. Bentley, who had died instantaneously, was also taken out. The dark little stranger did not speak, but his eyes were bright with fear.

Doc Little, his urgent work finished, looked at Mark.

'How did he get in?' he demanded.

'*I* don't know,' said Mark. He looked almost with reproach at his cousin. 'Didn't you see him?'

'He didn't come in by the street door,' said Mike.

'That's certain, sir,' volunteered a Special Branch man.

'He came to the front door of the flat,' said Mark.

'He didn't get in by a window or by the fire-escape,' said

Dunster, his curly hair rumpled and his round face sober. 'I'm quite sure of that.'

'Well, he got in somehow,' said Mark, rubbing his stomach gently.

'Not necessarily,' said Doc Little. 'I mean, not necessarily this morning, or since you've been watching the place.'

'We've been watching night and day,' said Mike.

'Well, then—'

A well-dressed woman who had come from the flat below volunteered the information that the stranger had been living in the building for a week—he had rented a furnished flat on the second floor, and lived there alone. There was some relief in the knowledge that there had been no negligence.

Loftus was in Craigie's office when Mark came to report. Loftus had just arrived from Bournemouth, and Craigie had done most of the talking. He had been there when the telephone call had come, and now he looked at Mark, his face expressionless, while Mark went through it all again, between intervals of rubbing his stomach, and carefully explained how the stranger had gained access.

'I ought to have stopped him,' Mark said. 'It was just that I didn't think anyone could get through—I wasn't awake.'

'Steady,' said Loftus. 'No self-reproaches, we've got too much to do. At least we know where the main leakage was.'

'That's about all,' said Mark dismally.

'It isn't quite all,' said Craigie. He went to the wash-basin, which was built into the wall, filled a kettle and put it on an electric ring. 'We've got Gertrude Ryall to watch. She certainly hasn't been seen with Rutter, or in Bournemouth, and she gives us the other line that we've been looking for. As for

Bentley—' He paused, and took his pipe from his lips. 'I think, on the whole, it was the best way out for him.'

'You haven't seen his sister,' said Mark.

'She'll come to that conclusion, too,' said Craigie. 'There was nothing but disgrace to face, and now there is a chance that her brother's name won't reach the Press. Members of the family have held high positions at Whitehall for centuries, it's a tradition. She herself is studying for the Diplomatic Service, and was at our Washington Embassy for some years.'

'How's Bruce?'

'Not seriously hurt,' said Loftus. 'He'll be all right in a few weeks. I'm sorry he's got to spend a time convalescing, we didn't want him brooding just now, but it might also do him good in the long run.' It was not callousness, it was a dispassionate review of the facts. Loftus, as well as Craigie, had learned to be dispassionate.

'How about Christine?' asked Mark.

'She's doing nicely,' said Loftus. 'Well out of danger.'

'Good!' Mark looked more cheerful. 'Well, where do we go from here?'

'Gertrude Ryall is our first quarry,' said Craigie. 'I hope to get some word about her soon. We've discovered where she lives in London—a small flat in a mews near Bentley's place— and we know that she had a flat in a house at Solihull, Birmingham. Both are being watched, of course. There's a report that a bearded man, perhaps Kelly, left the same house in Birmingham a few days ago,' said Craigie. 'We're having that checked. Everything considered, I think there's a fair chance of getting results soon.'

'Yes,' said Mark. 'I hope so.'

The green light showed in the mantelpiece, and Craigie leaned forward and pressed the knob beneath it. The door slid open, to reveal Mattley standing there with Mike Errol. The atmosphere grew tense; for there was no doubt that Mattley had bad news. He was obviously deciding on how best to deliver it.

'At least *you're* making progress,' he said, at last, but none of the others spoke. 'I have some grave news.'

Loftus shifted a little in his chair.

Mattley went on:

'Professor Gabriel Toller was attacked last night when he was taking a walk, escorted, near the experimental station where he is working. He was not killed, nor gravely injured, but he had with him the formula for T.N.25.'

Mike snapped his fingers, making a sharp report.

'That was stolen,' said Mattley. 'Moreover, the United States and the Russian Governments have received further approaches from the individual who first offered them the formula and gave them the information. He has sent them the *first half* of the formula, as an earnest of what is to come. It coincides, letter for letter, with the original—the original which Toller developed and which, we believed, only he and Dr. Morritz knew. So that the formula was seen *before* it was stolen from Toller.'

After a long pause, Loftus said:

'Pointless.'

'What is pointless?' Mattley looked at him.

'The attack on Toller,' said Loftus.

'Not necessarily,' objected Craigie. 'Morritz might have parted with half of the formula, so they might not have the rest.'

'I don't think that's likely,' said Loftus.

'I'll leave you to work on that,' said Mattley, standing up. 'Of course, Toller himself is largely to blame for this fresh mishap. He has constantly refused to take his danger seriously, in spite of the many attempts on his life.'

'Our efforts have been cancelled out,' said Loftus.

'I shouldn't take it quite as badly as that,' said Mattley. 'I know you will see this through, as you have seen so many other things through. *Nothing* must be allowed to prevent you.'

As he spoke a telephone rang. A mauve light shone in it. Craigie stood up. 'That's from Bournemouth,' he said, 'there might be some news, if you'd care to wait.'

'I will, thanks,' said Mattley.

Craigie went to the desk and answered the call. It was rarely possible to judge from Craigie's reactions whether news was good or bad, but to all of them it seemed that he stiffened and showed a faint hint of excitement.

'Yes,' he said. 'On no account lose her.' After a few more words he replaced the receiver and looked at the others, paused for a moment, and then said: 'Gertrude Ryall is in Bournemouth.'

'Well, well, *well*!' said Mark.

'Visiting *Chineside*, as Bentley did?' asked Mike.

'No, a different house. We might soon have firm news for you, sir,' he added, and Mattley gave a smile from which all touch of winter had gone, before he went out.

16

MORE MOVES IN BOURNEMOUTH

'W ell,' said Polly Dalton, 'it is a fact that Loftus has gone back to London, that there are only five men left here now, and that all I've been doing is to—'

'Loll in the sun with Uncle George,' said George Henry George, 'and I may tell you, my poppet, that many young girls would consider that a privilege.'

'I am not so young as all *that*,' said Polly, pointedly.

Bannister and Commyns had gone to a summer-house, where they were relaxing in the shade. The three other women, wives and friends of the Department men, had gone out shopping. Polly had been prevented from going with them by a palpable trick on George's part, who wanted her company.

Suddenly Hoffmann came out of the house, waving urgently.

'It's probably the telephone,' said George.

Polly followed him as he ran towards the house.

Hoffmann waited for Polly on the steps, smiled, and

walked in with her. From the small private lounge, George's voice was coming, and Hoffmann was looking towards him.

'Yes,' said George. 'By St. Jeremiah, *will* I!... Yes, right away... Give me the address again... Meyrick Park... . Yes, I've got it.' He replaced the receiver, and as they entered the room he clapped his hands 'Zip-peeee!' he cried. 'Work for the slaves!'

'For me?' asked Polly, quickly.

'Soon, I expect,' said George, hopefully. 'Not this time. Sorry, old girl, but you know how it is—orders, as they say. But if you would like to do something, my poppet, hop round and tell Bannister and Commyns that there is work to be done.'

'What work?' asked Polly.

'One Gertrude Ryall, of beauty unsurpassed, known to be mixed up in this most unholy mix-up, is in Bournemouth,' said George. 'We're all out for Gerty!'

Polly went to fetch the others.

George smiled at Hoffmann, who moved the fingers of both hands at great speed, in sign language, his eyes grown brighter. Before Polly and the others had returned, Hoffmann was on his way along the drive.

George beamed at Bannister and Commyns.

'You've heard about Gertrude? She's at a house called *Rostrum*, near Meyrick Park Crescent. Two of the lads followed her from Bournemouth. Our job is to make sure that we find out all there is to know about *Rostrum*. Loftus wants one of us to tackle the helpful Mr. Mildmay, one to see Superintendent Carr, the others to find a way to the house. Hoffy's on his way there.' He paused, and frowned. 'My Polly, there *is* work for you. Who could win Mildmay so winsomely as winsome Polly? Do you know where his office is?'

'I noticed it near the Square,' said Polly.

'You've a nose for this business,' said George. 'Will you hop down and see him? Make an appointment by telephone first, and give Loftus's name. Very urgent. Yes?'

'Yes,' said Polly, eagerly, and started down the drive.

'Well, you needn't take your racquet with you,' said George, 'and the telephone's inside.'

'There's a call-box at the corner,' said Polly. She put her racquet against a deck-chair and hurried on.

'I'm going to keep an eye on Polly,' said George, 'will you two look after the rest?'

'I'll do Carr,' said Bannister, 'and come along to *Rostrum* afterwards.

Commyns nodded. They went into the house to get automatics, which they pocketed with as little fuss as if they were cigarettes, and hurried off.

George reached the kiosk as Polly was hurrying from it towards the Square. He followed her at leisurely pace. He had not told her, but several times they had noticed that Polly had been followed wherever she went. George did not like it, and wished she had left Bournemouth. It was never by the same man, and he had not sent a report to Craigie about it, feeling that he had too little justification. He might, he knew, be right in his surmise, but the follower might be no more than a young man who hoped to pick up an acquaintance. Most of the men whom he suspected had been young and, apparently, on holiday.

Thinking on those lines, George watched her cross the Square and hurry into the offices of Mildmay, Drew and Mildmay. As he did so a rather elegant young man reached the window and looked at the photographs of the houses— across most of which was pasted a red slip, saying 'sold'. George's eyes narrowed, for that elegant young man had shown interest in Polly before.

The young man went into the agent's doorway.

Meanwhile, Polly sat opposite the gentle Mr. Mildmay.

Of course he remembered Mr. Loftus—a very amiable gentleman, who had inspired the statement, issued to the local as well as the national Press, that the landslide at Alum Chine had been caused by an experiment with high explosives, an accident which would not occur again. This had pleased Mr. Mildmay, whose main concern was the good name of Bournemouth, and the assurance that nothing would allow the rumour to spread that the chines were unsafe. Did not Miss Dalton think them beautiful?

'Very,' said Polly, jumping at the chance to get a word in. 'Marvellous! Mr. Mildmay, Mr. Loftus said that you had been so helpful, and knew so much about Bournemouth, that perhaps you could give him a little more information.'

'If I can, it is at his disposal,' said Mildmay.

'Thank you *so* much. There is a house called *Rostrum*, near Meyrick Park. Do you know who owns it?'

It was almost impossible for Mr. Mildmay to register consternation, so mild was his manner, but he could and did show surprise. He hesitated, and then said slowly: 'Is Mr. Loftus in Bournemouth?'

'No, in London, but he telephoned an urgent message.'

'I suppose I *am* right in divulging this information,' said Mildmay. 'In any case, you can find it out elsewhere, and you are such a determined young lady that I know you would not lose time! Mr. Hemmingway Noel bought *Rostrum*.'

'Who is he?' asked Polly.

Mildmay coughed, from sheer amazement.

'Surely you know that he—well, he is a *well*-known figure, Miss Dalton? A very wealthy man. *Very* wealthy.' There, undoubtedly, was Mr. Mildmay's weak spot; he venerated wealth. 'Haven't you heard of Hemmingway, Noel and

Hemmingway? My dear young lady, it is on a par with Vickers, the B.S.A. and other great—'

'Armament firms!' exclaimed Polly.

'They are now turning their attention to the manufacture of goods for more peaceable purposes, I am glad to say,' said Mildmay. 'I have that from Mr. Hemmingway Noel himself. I cannot help feeling that Mr. Loftus is wrong to think that *Rostrum* is worthy of his attention.'

Polly did not commit herself. 'Do you know how long he has been at *Rostrum*? Mr. Noel, I mean.'

'About six months,' said Mildmay. 'I *could* tell you the exact date, if you think it will help.'

'I don't think that matters,' said Polly. 'We can get it later, if needs be.' She felt greatly excited, but there was a streak of caution in her, something which George and Loftus had noticed before. She was surprisingly shrewd, and it occurred to her that Mr. Mildmay was remarkably distressed at the mention of *Rostrum*. *She must remember to tell George that.*

'Does Mr. Noel take any part in local affairs?' she asked.

'Indeed he does—a most gratifying interest. He has already made gifts of considerable sums to local charities. I certainly hope that Mr. Loftus has made a mistake.'

'He might have done,' conceded Polly. 'Thank you very much. Mr. Mildmay.'

'Oh, that is perfectly all right,' said Mildmay.

He looked a little dazed as Polly went out.

She was frowning, and the frown deepened when she noticed the man standing at the counter of the outer office. He was an elegant young man in grey flannels, a blazer with a colourful badge and a silk square, tied choker-fashion. He smiled diffidently at her. She ignored him, and went out. She did not think there was much more that she could learn about this mysterious

Mr. Noel. If he were a partner in Hemmingway, Noel and Hemmingway, Loftus and the man Craigie, of whom she had heard a great deal, would know where best to get the information.

Armaments—and a high explosive; obviously there was a connection. She wished she could hurry back to *The Pines*, but probably no one would be there to telephone London. She had not been told the London telephone number, and she had hesitated to ask for it.

'Excuse me,' said a man, gently.

He touched her arm, and in his hand was a handkerchief. He was the elegant young man, with a rather timid smile and a somewhat boyish face.

'I think you dropped this,' he said.

'I don't think so,' said Polly.

'Oh! Oh, I'm sorry.' The young man stood staring at her, rather shamefaced. He looked so shy that her suspicions, aroused when he had touched her arm, disappeared completely. 'I quite thought you had. Er—I have seen you in Bournemouth several times, I think.' They had started to walk together towards Old Christchurch Road, a one-way turning. Traffic flashed by, an old man skipped out of the way of a motor-cycle that was travelling too fast, and turned to mutter angrily after the driver.

The young man walked on the inside of the pavement. Polly did not notice it. She was a little embarrassed; she disliked such casual meetings, but she always found it hard to administer the *congé*.

'It *is* a bore being on one's own, isn't it?' said the young man, hopefully. 'I was to have come here with friends, but they could not get away at the last moment, and I could not rearrange my holiday. Er—'

A powerful lorry roared up Old Christchurch Road. A man

passed Polly's companion, apparently making him lurch against her. She had to step into the road.

'Oh, I'm so sorry!' he said. 'That lorry was too near the kerb.' He glanced behind him. A powerful car was swinging round the bend in the road. '*Much* too near,' he said—and then he lurched against her again, and this time made her lose her balance.

Someone screamed!

It was all done so quickly that Polly did not realize what was happening. One moment she was falling into the road, the next an arm shot out and sent her back to the pavement. Polly did not see George Henry George leap from the road, or the wing of the car brush against him, or the startled face of the diffident young man.

George gripped the young man's arm.

'Little man,' he began, 'I think—'

'Little man' eluded his grip, and drove his fist towards his stomach. George saw the blow coming, parried, and put over a straight left which the young man evaded with a skilful move-ment of his head. A policeman came up, booming: '*Now*, then!' A man put a restraining hand on George, and the young man with the scarf took advantage of that to slip away.

'Now, then—'

George said: 'Look after my lady friend, please.'

He side-stepped the policeman, handed off another man who decided that he could be of service by getting in his way, and raced up the street. Turning left, he saw the grey flannels and the blue blazer disappearing in the direction of the Square. George reached the end of the road in time to see him board a taxi, which was pulling out from a rank near the Lower Pleasure Gardens. No other taxi was near.

'Oh, lord!' exclaimed George.

The taxi disappeared near the Town Hall, and George

muttered: 'Meyrick Park and *Rostrum*, for a fortune. Well, the others will know.'

He was quite right.

The young man's taxi swung into the drive of *Rostrum* and the young man jumped out, flung a ten-shilling note at the taxi-driver and curtly told him to get away, then ran up the steps leading to the imposing front door of *Rostrum*. It was a modern house, large, impressive, built of yellow sandstone and yellow brick. The grounds were superb; a gardener was working on a lawn in which there were many rose-beds.

In a shrubbery were two Department men, and near the side of the house, hidden by bushes, was Hoffmann. Commyns, so dark and saturnine, was walking outside.

The young man burst into the hall, and a manservant appeared.

'Where's Mr. Noel?' demanded the young man.

'I think he is in the study, Mr. Thomas, with Miss Ryall.' The manservant looked his disapproval as Thomas ran up the wide staircase, jumping the last few stairs, swung right and then, without knocking, flung open the door of a large, sunlit room. A man and a woman, standing near the window and very close together, looked round in surprise.

'What's this, Thomas?' demanded Noel, abruptly. 'Why didn't you knock?'

'There isn't time for ceremony,' said Thomas, breathlessly. 'Listen to me—'

17

THE DISAPPEARANCE OF
'THOMAS'

Hemmingway Noel looked down on the young man from a height of six feet three. He had an expression of contempt which sat ill on a face that was usually composed, genial, even benevolent. He was a man of forty who had made a cult of benevolence. Even those friends who knew much of his real activities, were deceived—Noel, they thought, never took a decision unless he believed it right. It was the duty, Noel often said sententiously, of every Englishman worth his salt to see that England was never again without arms. Better still, they should carry out experiments unceasingly, should perfect the methods of production, should have in their hands the power which would make other nations wilt.

Could one believe, Noel would murmur in his quiet, impressive voice, that America had *no* imperialistic ambitions?

Could one believe, Noel would inquire in a still quieter voice, that the Union of Soviet Russia had none?

Now his bold eyes were glinting and his lips were set tightly, as if he had the greatest difficulty in keeping silence. Gertrude Ryall, standing by the window, looked at him with a faint frown. The sun caught her golden hair, her fair skin, her large eyes, grey-green, with their colour brought out by the slightest touch of mascara. Well groomed, sleek, lovely—if one believed that loveliness was a matter only of form and figure.

Thomas looked distressed.

'Well, aren't you going to say something?' he demanded.

'My *dear* Thomas,' said Hemmingway Noel, in a voice which was syrupy with sarcasm, 'I think you have done a wonderful job. Oh, wonderful! You heard the girl talk to Mild-may, and instead of telephoning me from the nearest call-box you indulged in a fantastic orgy of violence engaged in a bout of fisticuffs with this young man who attacked you, and then—your *crowning achievement*, Thomas!—you came straight here.'

Thomas licked his lips.

'Now look here, Hem—'

'Undoubtedly my greatest mistake was in thinking you had a spark of intelligence,' said Noel. 'Now, Thomas! Take the car—the small car. Put in enough things for one night. Get as far away from here as you can.'

'But—'

'Get out!' cried Noel.

The young man, open-mouthed, saw something in the older man's eyes which frightened him. He backed towards the door, casting an appealing glance at Gertrude. She offered no sympathy. He kicked against the door with the back of his foot, and went out. He stood still for a moment in the passage, trembling, and wiping his forehead. It was damp again almost as soon as he took his handkerchief away.

Inside the room, Gertrude said:

'The young *fool*!'

'I think perhaps you would have been wiser to stay away

from here, too,' said Noel, coldly. 'Go into the small room, Gertrude.'

'Hem, I—'

'I really cannot talk to you now,' said Noel. 'This is an emergency.' He did not smile as he took her arm and led her to a door, which he opened and pushed back. She looked at him with a sideways glance, and then went into the other room. He closed the door, and she felt a little shaken. A moment before Thomas had burst into the room, she had been prepared to exult; Noel seemed so completely hers.

Now she was far from sure.

Noel stepped to the telephone, which was on a table in a corner of that book-lined room.

'Give me Mr. Bradd,' said Noel.

He waited for a moment, while the operator, who was always on duty at the small private exchange in *Rostrum*, put him through to 'Mr. Bradd'. Rutter answered him.

Noel said: 'Thomas has led them here. He is leaving in a few minutes. I doubt whether he will get more than twenty miles away. Do you understand?'

Twenty-five minutes later, passing through Ferndown, a large, rambling residential village on the outskirts of Bournemouth, a small sports car was travelling at high speed— such high speed that people stopped and stared aghast. The small car, with Thomas at the wheel, swung right into the Ringwood Road, and, a few hundred yards along, blew up.

Loftus heard about the young man only twenty minutes after George had made sure, from Commyns, that Thomas had entered the drive of *Rostrum*. At that time Thomas had not yet driven away. Five minutes afterwards Loftus had another urgent call from George. George had returned to *The Pines* and telephoned, and, coming away from the instrument, seen Polly hurrying up the drive. There was a bruise on her chin and a scratch on the back of her hand, but apart from those things she was unhurt.

'George!' she cried. 'George—Hemmingway Noel lives at *Rostrum!*'

'Does he, by George!' said George, and before she had reached him, he was at the telephone again.

In Craigie's office, Loftus watched Craigie lift the receiver of the telephone connected by private wire to *The Pines.* Craigie pointed to a telephone on another desk, and Loftus went to it to listen in. George was brief and to the point; should he take immediate action to see that Noel did not escape?

'Yes,' said Craigie. 'Get in touch with Superintendent Carr. Ask him to lend you what men you need. If Noel should leave the house, ask him to go back. If he refuses, detain him.'

'My, *my!*' said George. 'The great big Noel and me! Right-ho, old chap.'

He rang off, turned round and took Polly's arms, and danced a jig with her. She was laughing when he had finished. He swung round again to the telephone and put a call in to Superintendent Carr, who promised immediate help.

'That man ought to get a medal,' said George. 'I used to think that Bournemouth people were obstructive. That reminds me, how are you?'

'Oh, I'm fine,' said Polly. 'Thank you *so* much for your kind inquiry. What did they ask me to do?'

'Take the greatest care of yourself,' said George. 'You're precious. Pink, plump and precious!' he cried, and, quite unexpectedly, kissed her.

Then he hurried down the drive.

Polly stood looking after him, thoughtfully. Her cheeks were their usual pink, with no deeper flush, although one would have expected Polly Dalton to be indignant at such a liberty. By the time George disappeared, she was smiling.

Ten minutes later three large, plain-clothes men arrived at *The Pines*. George had made sure that Superintendent Carr took no chances with his Polly.

By that time, Loftus and Craigie were on their way to Heston Airport, and a small passenger aircraft was warming up to take them to Bournemouth.

George, a rather disappointed man, was waiting near the drive gates of *Rostrum*. There were two or three other men in sight, all dressed as if they were on holiday, and by no means remarkable. Occasionally people passed, but *Rostrum* was not on a main road; the tree-lined road it faced was not a widely used thoroughfare.

A car pulled up, and Loftus looked out of the window. Craigie was with him.

'Nothing doing,' said George.

'What do you mean?' asked Loftus.

'No scare for the gentleman,' said George. 'He has spent the last half-hour walking round the garden, admiring the roses. You would think his only interest in life was the way the petals grow, and aren't the scents wonderful? He had a bee-ootiful young lady with him.'

'Who?' asked Loftus.

'Known, of course, as Gertrude,' said George. 'He's shown no alarm, made no attempt to get away, no attempt to hide that Gertrude Ryall is with him. Between you and me,' added George, 'That man's a deep 'un.'

'*No!*' said Loftus, solemn-faced.

'All right, I asked for it,' admitted George. 'I say, can I come too? Into the lion's den, I mean. Valuable experience, seeing the great men at work. And after all,' continued George, ghoulishly, 'you never know when you might be bumped off, and I'll have to take your place.'

'Hop in,' said Loftus, when Craigie nodded.

When he had walked round the garden with his lady, Noel had given no indication that he knew that his shrubberies harboured men who were closely watching the house, and he did not turn a hair when the butler came in and presented Craigie's card—the one with Police and Home Office authority. He was sitting in the library with Gertrude, drinking iced lager.

He exchanged glances with her.

'We have aroused the interest of the police, my dear,' he said. They were on good terms again. 'Will you stay? They are remarkably interesting, I believe—quite incredibly stupid at times.'

'I'd like to stay,' said Gertrude. She sat back and pulled her skirt so that her long, shapely legs, encased in finest nylon, could hardly fail to attract the admiring attention of anyone coming into the room. She wore a white silk blouse and a grey pleated skirt, and looked delightfully cool—a charming lady!

'Show Mr. Craigie in, Croom,' said Noel, 'and take away this tray and glasses.'

'Very good, sir,' said the butler.

He went out. Soon Loftus and Craigie entered, and behind them came George, looking like a clown. He was untidy, his rather thin hair was dishevelled, and he still bore the marks of his brief encounter with Thomas. His broad grin made him look a little vacant, and when he saw Gertrude Ryall he stared

—first at her face and then at her knees. She could hardly restrain a smile at such *naïveté*.

Noel stood up.

'Good afternoon, gentlemen. Which of you is Mr. Craigie? Or should I say Inspector Craigie?'

'Just Mister,' said Craigie, and George nodded his earnest agreement. 'This is Mr. Loftus—and Mr. George.'

'Hallo,' said George, brightly.

He puzzled Noel, who gave him more attention than the others.

Noel towered over Craigie, and was almost as tall as Loftus, though the Department man seemed twice his size. He forgot to offer them chairs.

Loftus limped to one, and sat on the arm.

Noel raised his eyebrows.

'Sit down, please,' he murmured.

Craigie remained standing, and did not immediately speak. George stole another glance at Gertrude, and then looked blankly into Noel's face. Loftus and Craigie were watching the armament king steadily. Although Noel retained his set smile, it was growing a little strained, and when next he spoke there was an edge to his voice.

'Why have you come, Mr. Craigie?'

Craigie said: 'You have a nephew named Thomas Noel, I believe.'

'Oh, is this about Tom?' asked Noel. 'What has he been up to?' He sent a smiling glance at Gertrude. 'I knew he had been playing the fool when he came rushing in.'

Gertrude shrugged her shoulders and again attracted George's attention. George was glad that he had maintained the silly-ass technique for that interview. Noel's manner was remarkably cool—so cool and natural that it was difficult to believe that he was harbouring any guilty secret. The coolness of the girl was equally astonishing.

'What happened when he came in?' asked Craigie.

Noel walked to a table, took a cigarette, lit it, and flicked the match out of the open window. He did not offer cigarettes to any of the others.

'Really, Mr. Craigie,' he said, as if he were talking to a child, 'I cannot admit your right to question me in such a fashion. If you will have the goodness to explain why you have come, I will—if I think fit—help you.'

'I have come for several reasons,' said Craigie. 'Do you want me to detain you, Mr. Noel?'

'Detain *me*?' exclaimed Noel, but his expression was derisive.

'My dear Mr. Noel,' said Craigie, so well mimicking Noel's manner that George was unable to restrain a genuine smile, 'I have not come here from London for the sake of exchanging pleasantries. I have the authority to take you under arrest, and unless I have full co-operation from you, I shall do so.'

'Kindly explain yourself,' said Noel, haughtily.

Craigie took from his pocket a folded piece of paper, opened it, and handed it to Noel. It was a warrant for Noel's arrest.

It shook Noel.

'I shall demand an explanation of this,' he said, and the words sounded trite. 'In fact I will telephone the Home Office at once. You are exceeding your authority, Mr. Craigie.'

'Not my authority,' said Craigie, 'that of the State. Are you prepared to answer *any* questions which I put to you, Mr. Noel?'

'I'm damned if I will!' said Noel. He was shaken, and had lost a little of his poise, thought George delightedly. Easy game!

'You will be wise to,' said Craigie. 'What happened when your nephew came in?'

Noel said: 'He hurried in, blurted out something about having to return to London, and rushed out again. My butler tells me that he left in his car, not very long ago.'

'How long?' asked Craigie.

'A little more than two hours,' said Noel, and Craigie glanced at George, who nodded vaguely.

'Did he say what had happened?' asked Craigie.

'He attempted to,' said Noel, 'but I gave him no opportunity. I was engaged with Miss Ryall, and annoyed at the interruption. He did not wait.'

'Were you on good terms with him?' asked Craigie.

'On reasonably good terms,' said Noel. 'He is a young fool, in some ways. He runs through money like water, and—' He stopped abruptly.

'And what?' asked Craigie.

'I see no point in the question,' said Noel, coldly. 'I do not see *why* you should come here in this domineering fashion, or why you show such interest in my nephew. Some explanation is called for, don't you think?'

'Yes,' said Craigie. 'Later.'

'No, now!' snapped Noel, looking really angry. 'I will not submit to this insufferable interrogation a moment longer. If that paper you showed me is genuine, act on it. *I* will soon show you that making an arrest without good reason is not a thing to be recommended.'

'But I would have an excellent reason if I arrested you, Mr. Noel,' said Craigie, gently. 'You would be charged with conspiracy to obstruct the police, giving shelter to a person for whom there is a warrant for arrest—and sundry other offences.' He smiled. 'I don't think even your prestige and position would be of very much help.'

'Damn your insolence!' snapped Noel.

It was not going at all as Noel expected, thought George.

'Damn my insolence if you like,' said Craigie. 'Your nephew is suspected of complicity in a grave crime.'

'Are you accusing me of harbouring *him?*' demanded Noel.

'No.' said Craigie. 'You have been suspected of harbouring a known criminal, by name Arnold Rutter.'

'I know no one called Rutter,' said Noel.

'Perhaps not,' murmured Craigie, 'but he might have used other names.' He took another slip of paper from his pocket, and said: 'Read that, Mr. Noel. It is a search-warrant. I propose to search your house, here and now—unless, of course, you have any cogent objections.'

18

GERTRUDE RYALL

N oel raised no objections, beyond another 'damn your insolence'. If that were ever brought up as a point against him, or if a court wanted an explanation of his remarkable attitude to Craigie, as a police officer, doubtless Noel would say that he was angry but that in face of the warrants there was nothing he could do.

George Henry George was puzzled, and admitted it.

He could not see where Craigie was going—the arguments so far seemed largely pointless. Of course, they were intended to shake Noel's confidence; they certainly seemed to be succeeding in that. They might, too, be directed against the woman. She had not moved, not turned a hair, and her confidence seemed even greater than Noel's. In fact the man was not quite confident enough.

'A queer business,' George reflected.

Craigie sent him with a message for Superintendent Carr, who was downstairs, and then the search of *Rostrum* started. George went back to the library, where the other four were sitting or standing, looking at each other or looking into space. A curious show altogether, reflected George again. He was not at all sure that Craigie had not gone rather too far. Was he justified in riding the high horse like this? Hadn't Noel some protection in law?

Noel spoke suddenly.

'You will find no one here who has no right here—no one in whom the police need have any interest.'

'We'll see,' said Craigie.

'I will not permit this outrageous business to proceed for another minute!' roared Noel, and it seemed clear that he was close to breaking-point. 'I would have expected more consideration than most people, but at least I can insist on my right as a citizen! Explain your actions, Craigie, or—'

'Or what?' murmured Craigie.

Loftus said: 'Let's be done with it, Gordon, and take him away, He hasn't a leg to stand on.'

Noel swung round on him.

'I'll show you whether I've a leg to stand on! I will make sure that you're reduced to the ranks, I—'

'Nonsense,' said Loftus. 'Why make an even greater fool of yourself?'

'Fool!' gasped Noel. 'Fool!' He was trembling a little and there were beads of perspiration on his forehead. Now he was really alarmed. 'Why, I will make you suffer for this if I have to spend—'

'Your last penny?' murmured George.

He saw it clearly enough now, of course; they were prepared to take any steps to make Noel lose his temper, and the man was showing up badly now. His poise had gone, he had descended to bluster, which must be a new experience for the polished Hemmingway Noel.

Noel swung round on George, with his hand raised and clenched. Loftus and Craigie watched him hopefully.

Then Gertrude stood up.

'Don't let them rile you, Hemmy,' she said. 'You can deal with them later.'

Loftus silently cursed the woman. Only that quick, quiet warning was needed to bring Noel back to normal. He looked at her, ran his hand across his forehead, and then, backing to the window, summoned a wry smile and said:

'Yes, of course. All right, Mr. Craigie. Put on the handcuffs!'

'That will be done when we have heard the result of the search,' said Craigie. 'Now, Mr. Noel—how long have you known Miss Gertrude Ryall?'

The question startled them both.

'For many years,' Noel said, 'but if you think I am going to answer questions about Miss Ryall, you're mistaken.'

'I appear to be mistaken about a number of things,' said Craigie, quietly. He looked at the woman. 'Have you known Mr. Noel for a number of years?'

'Yes.'

'How many?'

'Six or seven years,' she said.

'In what capacity?' asked Craigie.

'That,' said Gertrude, 'is my business.'

Craigie smiled. 'I wonder if it is. How long have you known Mr. Hubert Wilberforce Bentley?'

The question did not come as a surprise to her, although she gave the three watching men the impression that she had to pull herself together before she answered.

'About four months,' she said.

'In what capacity?' asked Craigie.

'Must I ask the police whom I select as my friends?' she asked, sweetly.

'Mr. Bentley might have been well advised to do that,' said

Craigie, and George smothered a grin behind his large hand, for Craigie was now trying to break Noel's self-restraint by working on the woman. Craigie was masterly!

'I don't understand you,' said Gertrude.

'Is rudeness an *essential* part of police training?' demanded Noel, sneeringly.

'Bluntness often is,' said Craigie. 'Miss Ryall, a short time ago Mr. Bentley, at your request, obtained some papers from his office and gave them to you. What was the consideration?'

She snapped: 'It is not true.'

'It is supported by all the necessary evidence,' said Craigie. 'Denials will not serve you. What payment was made for those documents?'

'I saw no documents! Bentley and I were good friends,' she said, and then, with a recovery which had to be admired, much though Craigie regretted it, she went on: 'If you must know, we were engaged to be married. I broke the engagement some weeks ago—much against his wish.'

'Why did you?' asked Craigie.

Gertrude said, sweetly:

'Mr. Bentley was in financial difficulties, and while I was quite prepared to help him as far as I could, he would not accept gifts from me. The situation was a great trouble to him. He told me that he knew one way in which he could get money, and hinted at the possibility of selling information which was in his hands because of his position. I persuaded him to do nothing of the kind. If—' Her eyes widened, and she took a step towards Craigie. 'So he *has* sold them!'

Noel said: 'Have you come here to find State documents, Craigie? Good lord! I can understand your attitude now. I readily apologize if I was offensive.' He actually smiled charmingly, for there was no doubt that he was elated at the way Gertrude had said her carefully pre-arranged piece. 'That's a bird of another colour. Oh, and of course—that explains your Home Office authority. Frankness from the beginning would have been a much greater help, you know.'

'Possibly,' said Craigie. 'So your nephew came here, you refused to listen to what he said, and he hurried out. Meanwhile, Miss Ryall, you knew that Mr. Bentley was thinking of making capital out of State secrets, and broke your engagement because of it. Is that so?'

'There *are* limits,' said Gertrude, with a shrug.

'Yes,' said Craigie. 'Limits to our credulity, also. I don't believe a word of it.'

He startled them, but did not make them lose their composure.

There was a moment of silence, and before anyone spoke there came a tap at the door. Superintendent Carr entered. It was impossible for Carr wholly to hide the respect he had for the millionaire, and he looked a little awkwardly at Noel.

Noel said: 'Are *you* a party to this outrage, Carr? I thought you would have more sense. What have you found in my house?'

'Nothing,' said Carr.

Noel laughed; there was a high-pitched note in his laugh, as if he were relieved beyond measure but trying not to show it.

'You see,' he said, triumphantly. 'I will accept your apologies, Mr. Craigie!'

'No apologies,' said Craigie. 'I must ask you to come to London with me, Mr. Noel.'

Noel stared. 'Are you *mad*?'

Gertrude snapped: 'You have no reason to arrest Mr. Noel. No one has been found here, he is sheltering no one!'

'That may be true,' said Craigie, who looked disappointed. 'If I am putting you to trouble and inconvenience unnecessarily, Mr. Noel, you can have redress later. This is a matter under the Official Secrets Act, and you are needed for questioning—you, and Miss Ryall. How long will it take you to get ready?'

'I will not leave this house,' said Noel, now really worried.

'I do not want to use force,' said Craigie.

George, who had admirably placed his role of spectator, looked from the man to the woman, and he came to the conclusion that after their early triumph they had felt quite safe—and that the new shock was too much for them. The woman showed it more than Noel. He knew now, without any shred of doubt, that she had been acting. It had taken great will-power to maintain her poise, but now she was beginning to crack. Noel shot an anxious glance towards her, as if he expected it.

They had been in the room a little more than half an hour, and Noel thought: 'In another half an hour there will be no trouble from her.'

He said: 'We had better humour them, I suppose.'

'That is wise of you,' said Craigie.

'I have some small business matters which need immediate attention,' said Noel. 'May I have your permission to attend to them?'

'How long will they take?' asked Craigie.

'Not more than half an hour,' said Noel.

'All right,' said Craigie.

'You will leave me alone, I hope.'

'I shall not,' said Craigie.

Noel stared at him, and then shrugged his shoulders. He went to a bureau desk, pulled out a drawer, and put some papers on the desk. Most of them were accounts, and he signed cheque after cheque, tossing them into a small tray. He did not once look round. Carr, a little uncertain of himself, watched him, while Craigie and Loftus looked out of the window and George kept glancing at Gertrude Ryall. It was a bad show, thought George, not half as successful as it might have been. Noel had twice been on the point of breaking down, but had just saved himself.

There was no doubt of the tension under which he was working now.

The woman kept looking at him.

While Noel worked, a policeman came up to *Rostrum* and spoke to a plain-clothes man on duty outside. The plain-clothes man looked first surprised and then excited, told the policeman to take his place, and hurried into the house. Croom the butler was in the hall, puzzled and worried. He had been asked whether he had ever seen a man answering Rutter's description and, quite truthfully, he had said 'no'. That there was serious trouble was obvious to him.

'Where is Superintendent Carr?' the plain-clothes man asked him.

'In the study, I believe,' said Croom.

'Where's that?' asked the policeman, impatiently.

'I will show you up,' said Croom, with a long-suffering look, and led the way up the stairs. He tapped at the door, and George opened it. 'This gentleman wishes to speak to Superintendent Carr,' said Croom.

Carr stepped to the door.

'Will you have him in here?' asked Craigie.

Noel looked round, exasperated, then went on with his writing—he had signed thirty cheques, and now was reading some correspondence. As he looked round, he caught a glimpse of Gertrude's face. She was pale, and she held her hands close together, pressing the palms as if she were in pain. Loftus and Craigie had also noticed that something seemed to be the matter with her. Probably it was the strain of this interview.

The plain-clothes man came in, puffed up with self-importance.

'I thought you ought to know this at once, sir,' he said to Carr. 'The car in which Mr. Thomas Noel was travelling went through Ferndown, and then—'

Noel did not turn round, but he stopped reading. Craigie and Loftus watched him, George watched the woman. The plain-clothes man gave a nervous little cough, glanced at Noel, and then said:

'It blew *up*, sir!'

'Blew up?' ejaculated Carr.

'Without a trace, sir,' said the plain-clothes man.

Noel put down his pen, and turned round. His face was expressionless, but he could not keep the glint out of his eyes— and it was not a glint of regret.

'*What* did you say?' he asked, and the glint disappeared.

Carr, out of his depths, looked hard at him.

'I'm told that your nephew met with an accident—'

'It wasn't an accident,' said the plain-clothes man, importantly, 'It blew up! It didn't just crash or anything like that. Why, it disappeared!'

'This is nonsense,' said Noel. 'He—by George!' he exclaimed, and he had so schooled himself that the expression seemed one of genuine surprise. 'The little swine!'

'Sir!' ejaculated the plain-clothes man.

'The little *swine*!' repeated Noel. 'Craigie, why the devil didn't you catch him? I have had small quantities of a new explosive in the house, I was arranging for a trial at the gunnery school on the coast; Tom obviously stole it—'

'Stole it?' echoed Carr, faintly.

'He knew nothing about explosives,' said Noel. 'That particular type was in the experimental stage only, it would go off at a
certain heat, or if shaken severely. He must have had it in the car.'
He pushed his chair back and stood up, then without a word
hurried across the room towards a section of the book-lined
walls. He pressed a button, and the shelves moved out; behind
was a steel door. He worked the combination swiftly, pulled the
door open—it needed all his strength— and then stepped inside.

Craigie and Loftus followed him.

He took a small box from a shelf inside the strong-room; it
was so heavy that he needed both hands for it, and he gasped
as he carried it across the room. He put it on his desk, took
out a key, and opened the box.

Inside were two small compartments.

He said: 'Yes, it's gone. That explosive is so powerful that
we cannot yet control it—the utter fool!'

Craigie said: 'Why should he steal it?'

Noel glared at him, and said contemptuously:

'State secrets are not the only thing that can be sold at a
profit. That explosive is of enormous commercial value. Why,
if I could get my hands on him—'

'You would have to go rather a long way for that, it seems,'
said Craigie.

Noel said: 'If you think I am going to weep any tears for
my nephew, you are quite mistaken. I never trusted him. He
was too friendly with Dakers, much too friendly.'

'Dakers?' queried Craigie, while Loftus exchanged glances
with George. Dakers was a firm as well-known as Hemmingway, Noel and Hemmingway, and also made armaments.

'I hope I need not tell you who they are,' said Noel. 'I do
not propose to discuss my competitors with you, but Tom
probably thought he could sell to them. He would do anything

for money.' He paused, gradually widened his eyes, and looked at Gertrude. 'Didn't Tom know Bentley?' he asked her.

'Yes,' she said.

'It is beginning to look as if you did come to the right house,' said Noel, slowly. 'Ask Bentley what he sold to my nephew, Craigie, not to Miss Ryall.'

Craigie said: 'Bentley was murdered this morning.'

Noel said: "What? *Bentley* dead?'

It was perfect; in his own mind Craigie was quite convinced that this had been pre-arranged. He even suspected that Noel had pretended to get near breaking point so that this could be put over more convincingly.

Noel looked at Gertrude.

'Did you hear—' he began.

Gertrude stared at him wide-eyed—and her face was suddenly distorted, as if with pain. She gasped and raised her clenched hands in front of her, and then she slipped forward on her chair and fell to the floor.

19

POWER POLITICS

W ell,' said Loftus, 'what are you going to do?'
'I haven't decided,' said Craigie.

They were in a morning-room at *Rostrum*. Croom had just brought tea into them. Upstairs, Carr, George and a doctor were with Gertrude Ryall, who had not recovered consciousness.

'You're waiting to hear what happens to the woman, I suppose,' said Loftus. 'Is that right?'

'Yes,' said Craigie. He pushed his fingers through his hair, and added slowly: 'It's brilliantly done, Bill. Noel had little time to prepare the story, but it's almost water-tight.'

'It is water-tight,' said Loftus.

'No, there are some holes,' corrected Craigie. 'Young Noel came here, entered the study—we have the butler's word for that—and was there for ten minutes. Hole Number One—it doesn't square up with Noel's statement that he would not give his nephew any time to talk. Young Noel doubtless told him what had happened in the talk. Noel made sure that in the car was enough of the explosive to blow the car and his nephew to smithereens. The possibility that the explosion would happen in a built-up area did not worry him. Then he gave Gertrude a drink. We met the butler coming out with the glasses. Noel was afraid that she would crack. In the drink was the poison which has worked now, and I shall be surprised if she recovers. The glasses have been washed up, there's little chance of finding the proof that he poisoned her. Oh, we might,' he added, 'but—'

There was a tap at the door.

'Room for a little one?' asked George, and he sidled into the room. His eyes widened at the sight of the tea-tray. 'That's not friendly,' he said. 'Sneaking off for a quick one while I'm doing the heavy work. Er—here's a present for you.'

He held out a small glass phial, containing several tablets, greyish brown in colour.

'Where did you get them?' asked Craigie, looking at them intently. 'There's another cup—help yourself.'

'Thanks. The lady's bag,' said George. 'Sinister-looking things, aren't they? The doctor says that she died from irritant poisoning.'

'Died?' ejaculated Loftus.

'Yes,' said George, briefly. 'I was there. Nice chap, Noel. His nephew and his lady love could have given him away, and he didn't trust either. So he made Tom into a double-crosser and killed him, and he made Gertrude commit 'suicide'. Those tablets will be the poison tablets—care to bet?'

'No,' said Loftus.

'Wise man,' said George. 'Well, there it is. Er—I hesitate to make suggestions Guv'nor, but it might be a good idea to make Noel cough up the formula for this explosive.'

'Yes,' said Craigie.

'It will not be so easy,' said Loftus.

'Oh, we'll get it from him,' said Craigie. 'I think we shall find that he will turn right round, now, and pretend to be as helpful as he can. The danger for him has receded. So far as we know, there's only Rutter left, and Rutter might have slipped away.'

'The place was closely watched,' said George.

'We don't know for certain that Rutter has even been here,' said Craigie. 'From what we've heard from the servants, he hasn't been seen.'

'No,' said George. 'Deep in the doldrums, aren't we? Won't *any* of the beggars we've captured talk?'

'We'll try them again,' said Loftus, grimly.

'That's more like it! Er—Noel is throwing a fit of grief. Near to tears, you know the kind of thing. Distraught. Betrayed by his nephew, walked out on, in a manner of speaking, by his lady, he really doesn't know what to do next. Can I ask a question?'

'Go on,' said Craigie.

'Thanks. This is it: weren't you a bit too heavy-handed with Noel? I mean, can he kick up a stink?'

'Yes,' said Craigie, 'but that needn't worry us much.'

'A few questions in the House, I suppose,' said George. 'I was thinking, he has probably a lot of supporters at Westminster, millionaires do have, don't they? And—sorry about this, Guv'nor, but you know what it is. Old brain simmering, I can't let the steam off without an audience. We're rather sweating on trouble from the American Press, aren't we?'

'Yes,' said Craigie, thoughtfully. 'Go on.'

'English papers, please copy,' murmured George. 'They will. Great outcry. England playing at power politics, trying to develop new weapons, bang goes Atlantic Charter and unity of United Nations. Same like you said. Nasty for

Mattley and company, and then—out pops Noel's best parliamentary boy-friend from his burrow. Government using an unnecessarily high hand. Grave fear that the Government is showing distinct Fascist tendencies. Will power-drunk Prime Minister ever be stopped? Freedom and the rights of man, democracy—' He paused again. 'Need I go on?'

'No,' said Craigie. He was smiling faintly. 'Thanks, George. You've helped me to make up my mind.'

'No detention,' murmured George. 'Er—I know I'm talking out of place and all that kind of thing, but Noel will almost certainly give an interview to the Press. He will say what his Parliamentary friend would like to say. I mean, we *are* in a bit of a spot, aren't we?'

Loftus laughed.

'*Very* funny,' said George. 'Only I can't see the joke.'

Craigie said: 'We have gone fairly close to the wind before, George.'

'Ah, yes,' said George, 'but you can't pull the wool over my pretty eyes. No, sir. You're worried. So you should be. If this thing really blows to gale strength, then the Mattley administration is a thing of the past. What will the Department do then, poor thing? Clean sweep. Disbanded. There'll be much strong feeling, you know. In my quiet way,' added George, with a bright smile, 'I am a student of politics. I don't share some people's distrust of the Mattley administration, but this will be a prize packet for those who do.'

'You're not far wrong,' said Craigie.

Half an hour afterwards he left *Rostrum*, and the police were withdrawn from the house. Department agents who had come down from London, including the Errols, watched it by day and by night, but nothing happened for two days. Then Noel summoned to his home the representatives of the national daily papers, promising them a story of unusual importance.

The story was published next morning, with front page headlines and, in some cases, screaming leaders against the iniquitous Government. The whole story was brought out, Craigie was named as well as Loftus and several of the others. This sinister Department, the existence of which had been known to the Press for many years, must be closed down. It must be disbanded, there must be no delay. When a man of Noel's integrity, of such known service to the country, was treated in such an arbitrary manner...

And so on, and so on.

Not all the papers took that angle. Several of them gave veiled hints that the work of the Department had been of great value, that it was being made a scapegoat for a blunder which originated not with the Department but at Downing Street. The Prime Minister was a man of great courage: let him now admit that a blunder had been made. Let there be a formal apology to Hemmingway Noel in the House.

Then, on the same evening, came the Yellow Network broadcast from New York. The headline was 'Power Politics' and the announcer was so excited that at times he lost his breath. He was a well-known isolationist mouthpiece, with powerful backing, and there was no doubt that many sections of the American Press would support him next morning.

They did.

The story of the secret explosive was given in bald detail. Morritz and Toller were named, the explosion at Alum Chine was cited, dark motives implied. London had given no answer, said the Press in an excess of speculation, to the repeated requests from the State Department for information Britain could not be trusted. The Mattley administration stood condemned by its own actions. The duty of the United States was to make itself impregnable, and to let Britain and other countries murder each other if they wished.

It went on, *ad nauseam.*

Hemmingway Noel, still at *Rostrum*, was in a very good humour that day, and he sent to charities gifts totalling a hundred and ten thousand pounds.

There was an emergency meeting of the Cabinet.

There was an emergency meeting in Craigie's office, where Loftus, the Errols and several other agents gathered, and most of them looked glum.

There was, also, a smaller emergency meeting at *The Pines.* American papers had reached there by special messenger, and had been read and digested. The English papers had been scrutinized, line by line. None of the agents there liked to switch on the radio, for the B.B.C. was being remarkably frank in its relays of American opinion.

Red Star reported the uproar, without comment.

Pravda said that if the signatories to the United Nations' many agreements were not to be trusted, the U.S.S.R. had a number of significant devices which would be better kept at home than sent abroad.

George Henry George sauntered from the telephone into the large lounge at *The Pines* and beamed across at Polly, who was with Mark Errol's wife, a tall, dark-haired woman, rather quiet and undemonstrative.

'What-ho, Pink Polly,' said George. 'Care for a walk?'

'I'm going to see Christine.'

'Leave that to Mrs. Mark,' said George. 'She won't mind. She's a wonderful conveyor of good messages, too, aren't you, Mrs. Mark?'

Mark's wife laughed.

'And that reminds me,' said George. 'I've just had a tele-phone call from the Great White Chief, Craigie. Hammond is getting along nicely, thank you.' He lit a cigarette, and, step-ping to Polly, took one from her knee and another from her hair, lit one of them, and handed it to her.

'You *hopeless* fool,' said Polly.

'I resent the "hopeless",' said George. 'Polly, as you love all who are forlorn, come for a walk with me. I am serious. As a matter of fact,' he added, and there was a sudden change in his voice and in his eyes, 'I can't stay around here any longer, and if I go out alone I shall probably throw myself over the cliff. We haven't got a line of any kind now. We're just beat. Loftus has had a go at all the prisoners, and not a word has he got out of them. He's just telephoned me. Rutter has disappeared into thin air, and I—Come for a walk, Polly!'

'Will you mind going to the nursing home alone?' Polly asked Mark's wife.

'Of course not. Off with you,' said Mrs. Mark.

'Bless your big heart!' said George.

On the drive, he said soberly:

'I feel just as bad as I made out, this is not a trick. When I think of what Loftus and Craigie have tried to do, when I think how near we got to fixing Noel, and now this—it makes me want to cry!'

'They *can't* turn Mattley out now,' said Polly.

'Oh, can't they? And if it comes to that, why shouldn't they if they really don't like his politics? The thing is, to give him the boot on a count like this, when we know what he's been trying, when—Oh, never mind. Like an ice cream?'

'I suppose so,' said Polly.

'We'll go to that sumptuous emporium near the bus station,' said George. 'Bentley's sister Paula is going to see

Noel. I told you about her, remember? I don't know whether Loftus has got an idea that she can help, but she's coming down, and I'm to be outside *Rostrum* at half-past four. It's now nearly three. We have an hour and a half in which to make ourselves drunk on ice-cream sodas.'

'What are you going to do when you go there?' asked Polly.

'I haven't the faintest idea,' said George. He walked along in silence for a few minutes. They were at the top of the cliff, with hundreds of people passing them. Below, the sea was spotted with bathers, and near the pier the beach was so crowded that it looked as if the sand had gone dark and was seething like boiling water in a saucepan.

'George, why did you make a point of bringing me out?' Polly demanded, suddenly.

'Sinister motive,' said George. 'I mean it—really sinister. I hate it. Polly, you can still say no, you know.'

She stood quite still and looked at him, and she knew that he was not fooling now. He had brought her out with a firm purpose in mind, and that purpose helped to make him even more miserable and depressed.

'Go on,' said Polly.

'This is the position,' said George. 'We have twenty-four hours. There won't be a vote of confidence today, Loftus told me, there will be a debate in the House tomorrow. The censure motion, if it's coming, will come then. If it happens we can't do anything about it, our only hope is to have the whole truth for Mattley when he winds up the debate for the Government.'

'What has this to do with me?' asked Polly.

'You'll see,' said George. He was talking very quietly as they walked slowly on. 'If the Government falls it will be an admission to the world that we *have* been trying to put one across America and the Soviet Union. Everything we've tried to build

187

up will come down on us. It isn't an accidental set of circum-stances. It has all been well-timed. We know, although we can't yet prove, that Noel is in this business. Still, there's a fact we're apt to forget. Noel had to learn about T.N.25 from someone.'

Polly said: 'Was his nephew blown up by T.N.25?'

'Almost certainly,' said George. 'The point is, who told Noel about it? Where did he get the formula? Not from Morritz, who killed himself to save it. Hardly Toller, although possibly someone who worked with Toller when he was with Dakers. Who, then? Only the Cabinet and four officials besides Bentley knew of the stuff. We thought we'd solved that when Bentley cropped up, but we were wrong. Bentley changed the documents going to Washington and Moscow, but the formula was not in those documents. A Cabinet Minister might have had access, but—well, *someone* got hold of it before it was stolen from Toller the other day,' went on George. 'We stand or fall by our success or failure in finding out who first got that formula.'

'Yes, I can see all that,' said Polly.

'Good! The next item concerns you. Paula Bentley is going to tell Noel that *you* called several times at her brother's flat. We've been building you up gradually and very steadily. Noel, in spite of his success so far, must wonder whether we are going to spring a last-minute surprise. When Paula Bentley has left him, I think he will want to talk to you.'

'Oh,' said Polly.

'You can still say no,' George reminded her.

'I don't want to say no.'

'Polly,' said George, his voice very low.

'Yes.'

'You might never come out of that house,' said George.

'They can get you in—unless you back out of the business now—and there's no guarantee of what will happen afterwards.'

'Never mind that,' said Polly, recklessly. 'When I'm there, what am I to do? How can I help to make Noel give way?'

'As to that,' said George, slowly, 'I have instructions for you. Also, and oddly, I am coming with you.' He gave a sudden laugh, and squeezed her arm. 'Zounds! Are we downhearted? Listen...'

20

MR. RUTTER'S TRIUMPH

One of the features of *Rostrum* which had made Noel's choice fall upon it was the room below the house.

Mr. Mildmay knew nothing of that, for the Scotsman who had arranged for the building of the house for his own purposes had never mentioned it to the agent or architect. Why should he? The amiable Scotsman, however, had for some years been the chairman of a prominent firm of steel manufacturers, and for some reason a number of people equally interested in the manufacture of steel, and the things which were made of steel, often found it necessary to confer in a place where there was no fear of being overheard. There was nothing curious about this. The world of steel and its by-products, linked up with the world of explosives, and their by-products, and all the wide range of materials needed for the manufacture of armaments, was a different world from that of ordinary men.

This world, in fact, was international. In it, the real meaning of power politics was vested.

Not all the gentlemen interested in these raw materials,

products and by-products, were citizens of this world, however. Some—the great majority, in Gordon Craigie's opinion—were keenly aware of their obligations to the larger, brighter world which did not meet behind closed doors and soundproof walls in rooms approached by secret entrances.

In all, perhaps a dozen men knew of the room beneath *Rostrum*. Only Rutter, among them, was not a man of great wealth, and a leading figure in that other, sinister world.

The governments of the United Nations and the governments of those countries which were hoping, one day, to become members of the United Nations, knew of the existence of this nether world and, so far, had found no way in which it could be successfully invaded. What doubts they had consisted not of the existence of that world within a world but of the nations who knowingly sent representatives to it. The fear in the minds of many statesmen in America and in the U.S.S.R. was a real one: was Britain, in spite of her many eloquent protestations, subsidizing this small, compact and powerful community of persons—not one of peoples?

The room in Bournemouth where the denizens of the new underworld often met was approached through the strongroom at *Rostrum*. One stood by the far wall of the strongroom, after setting the mechanism in the study— mechanism which it was almost impossible to discover by chance—and a part of the wall opened. One stepped through the hole, and the wall closed behind. One began to descend, and the subdued light of the room below had a softening, restful effect.

Noel went down there at the time when Polly and George were talking so earnestly on the cliff.

He stepped into the room below. It was large and luxurious, with every conceivable appointment and convenience—

it was, in fact, one of a suite of three rooms, of which this was by far the largest.

Rutter rose from an easy chair, and put a book aside.

'In some ways,' said Noel, offering cigarettes, 'you are a remarkable man, Rutter. You could spend your life with books, tobacco, a little food and—solitude.'

'I have developed the habit of being alone,' agreed Rutter.

'And you have never told me why,' said Noel.

'That is not in our agreement,' said Rutter. The reluctant smile twisted his lips as he lit a cigarette. 'There is no need, now, why you should not know. I worked for Germany in the war. I was caught and sentenced to death. I was seriously ill after my trial and, of course, the humane authorities fought for my life and saved it, wanting me to be in the best of health when I died. By that time the war was over, and the sentence was commuted—I spent long years in a prison cell, compared with which this room is a palace. I learned to need little for my creature comforts. I learned to love books'—the word 'love' came oddly from those thin lips and in that harsh voice— 'and I learned to hate.'

'Your country?' murmured Noel.

'I hardly expected such patriotic nonsense from you,' said Rutter. 'I have no country and of all men, I think I hate Craigie most and Mattley next.'

Noel looked thoughtful: 'Why Craigie?'

'He caught me. I conceived a hatred for him when I first saw him, and nothing has lessened it. Much has strength-ened it.'

'Why Mattley?' asked Noel.

'I was earlier court-martialled for cowardice. He gave evidence against me. Whatever else, I have never been a coward.'

'Why did you start to work for us?' asked Noel.

'For a very simple reason,' said Rutter, and again the smile twisted his lips. 'You—everyone who has met in this room has good reason to fear Craigie and Department Z. We have worked together to destroy the Department—not to kill its members,' he added, slowly. 'There is no point in killing a man, it does not always make him suffer. And it is difficult, sometimes impossible, to make Craigie's men afraid. So I planned to hurt—first to attack them through their wives or through any person of whom they were fond. One of my men killed Hammond's wife. I tried to haunt all of them, one by one. I think, now, that some of them are frightened, not for themselves but for their womenfolk. Oh, they hide it well, but I have often thought of Loftus's feeling for his wife. If Peel had fired two inches lower—'

He broke off, and shrugged his shoulders.

'That is a matter which I have intended to discuss with you,' said Noel, and there was a silky note in his voice. 'What point was there in attacking Christine Loftus then? Was it to take personal revenge?'

Rutter laughed.

'You should know me better than to think I would give that first place. When I am working, I take what chance sends me gratefully, but the work is never neglected. I told Peel what to do for two reasons; to frighten the Dalton girl and to unnerve Loftus. Hammond has not been himself since his wife died; I think the death of Christine Loftus would have weakened the big man. They are easier to fight when they have something else on their mind—you will admit that.'

'Yes,' said Noel.

'I made it clear when you and I first worked together,' said Rutter, 'that of all the antagonists you were likely to meet, Craigie and his Department were the most formidable. I made it clear, and I had your full agreement, that if the Department could be wiped out, reduced to an ineffectual name perhaps, it would leave you a clearer road.'

'Yes,' said Noel. 'You were right.'

'Killing would not have served,' Rutter said again. 'You cannot reduce an organization like that by killing its members one by one. When one goes, another replaces him. I have watched the Department for many years. The way a leader is replaced is remarkable. Today, a man of whom you would think nothing at all if you passed him in the street or sat with him at dinner, shows much promise—or what Craigie would call promise.'

'Whom do you mean?' asked Noel.

'George—Henry—George,' said Rutter, with a pause after each name.

Noel looked startled. '*That* young fool?'

'I would not dismiss George as a young fool if I were you,' said Rutter. 'He has, however, a weakness—a great weakness. There is always something. He is fond of the Dalton girl.'

'I came to talk about her,' said Noel, 'but before I do— how do you force such loyalty from your workers, Rutter?'

Rutter said: 'Loyalty cannot be forced. I train them. Some I have selected because they are the type which can best be used, others because they already hate Craigie and all Craigie stands for. Kelly once worked against Craigie, and his daughter was killed. It was not, directly, the fault of Craigie or his men, if there was a fault it was Kelly's, but that did not matter to me. Maurice was once hunted high and low through Paris. He thinks that at least one of Craigie's men can name him as a collaborator.'

'Which one?' asked Noel.

'The little Jew, Hoffmann,' said Rutter. 'Maurice was in the internment camp office one day when Hoffmann was brought in for interrogation. What happened afterwards seems forgotten in Hoffmann's mind. Amongst other things, he lost his tongue for expressing his opinion of a highly placed German officer. When Maurice knew that Hoffmann worked for Craigie he was first afraid—and then elated.'

'And is now a prisoner,' said Noel, slowly.

'I do not think Maurice will talk freely, his hate is too deep,' said Rutter. 'Even if he talked, he could name no one but me. There is no need for alarm, I assure you. Now, please, what do you want to say about the Dalton girl?'

'How much does she know of what Craigie is doing?' asked Noel.

'I do not think she knows a great deal,' said Rutter, 'but undoubtedly George has told her something.'

'Would she know if Craigie is still watching me?' asked Noel, in a light voice.

'Yes. So do I. So do you.' Rutter smiled. 'He is!'

'The men have been withdrawn from the grounds,' said Noel, displeased.

'There are other points from which the house can be watched,' said Rutter.

'If that damned fool Thomas—' began Noel.

'Loftus would have got here without help from Thomas,' said Rutter. 'All the evidence goes to show that. The mistake, the greatest mistake, was in using Gertrude Ryall—yet I agree with you, it was difficult to choose anyone else, as Bentley was so completely in her hands.' Rutter seemed thoroughly to enjoy himself. 'If only they knew, the fools! Never has Craigie been so completely misled. Never has Loftus seen the obvious without realizing what it means. Oh, I have enjoyed this case very much, Mr. Noel—and I shall enjoy it more! I do not think that the Mattley administration will last more than another twenty-four hours—and that is also the measure of the life of Department Z. Imagine it! Craigie, Loftus, all the others, in possession of facts of vital importance, men trained into this work so that no others can rival them, and they have no counterpart in any part of the world—*dismissed.* Turned off unwanted—or found some sinecure, because the Treasury is still reluctant to dispense with the services of its staff.'

He paused for a moment, but Noel sensed that it was not a time to interrupt. He had known Rutter for many years, but never seen him so worked up, so tense, so filled with triumph.

'These men, such clever men, who know so much, whose knowledge is invaluable, whose experience might perhaps be called *vital* to Great Britain—imagine it!' cried Rutter. He laughed again, and it was an ugly sound. Then he said abruptly: 'What do you want me to do?'

'If the girl Dalton has much information—'

'She has little,' said Rutter. 'But George has a great deal, I think he is in Craigie's confidence. And the sure way to get him is to take the girl. He has followed her everywhere—as Thomas learned to his cost.'

'Can you get her?'

'Yes,' said Rutter. 'The question is not how to get them, but where to take them.'

'There is only one place,' said Noel. 'Here.'

'I do not agree with you,' said Rutter, firmly. 'You must not give them an opportunity to apprehend you on *any* count. You escaped before, thanks to your presence of mind. From now on you must work with great care, Noel, or you will find that you have made a fatal mistake.'

Noel said: "Where do you suggest?' He had paled and his eyes had narrowed, as if Rutter had given his self-confidence a sharp blow.

Rutter said: 'They do not expect me back at Alum Chine. Their men were taken from *Chineside* yesterday, for other work. It is still watched by the police, of course, and there are workmen in the chine. It would not do to go to *Chineside*, but there are several empty houses near by. We could use one of them. We can, with little difficulty, get the keys— one of my men can ask for an order to view, he will doubtless be trusted with the keys if he goes to Mildmays, shall we say, a little before they are due to close, and says that he wishes to see the house tonight. The order to view will be a great help, for we can first go to the house boldly.'

'I would hesitate to go myself,' said Noel.

'There is no need for you to come,' said Rutter. 'I can find out what George and the girl know.'

'You are very confident,' said Noel.

'I have good reason to be,' said Rutter, and he laughed. He paused, and a new expression crossed his face, one which puzzled Noel. Rutter went on slowly: 'They are remarkable people. I was once in a position, at the *Mayberry*, in which I thought my time had come. Then George let me go. I often wondered why. I went there because Merryweather was bungling his job.' He laughed again. 'How the dear Professor was nearly blown through the roof!'

Noel shrugged his shoulders.

'You have tried often enough to kill him, Rutter.'

Rutter looked at him, and rubbed his hands together.

'Yes,' he said. 'Yes!'

'And I think, pointlessly,' said Noel. 'Once we had the formula—which was *quite* your most successful effort—why did you worry so much about Toller?'

Rutter said: 'Don't forget the Department, Noel—you and I want to see the end of that. But I am wasting time,' he said. 'I must go out.'

Twenty minutes later Rutter, dressed in the uniform of a chauffeur at *Rostrum*, walked out of the garage. It was an excellent garage, with a car greasing-well. The walls of the well were not quite as solid as they seemed, and led to the room wherein was that sinister world.

When Rutter telephoned, a little after six o'clock, to tell Noel that he had the keys of a house near Alum Chine, Rutter found him in a state of some excitement.

'You were wrong about the Dalton girl,' Noel said. 'I have had a visit from Bentley's sister. Polly Dalton saw Bentley several times; Paula Bentley believes that the Dalton girl is working *against* Craigie. *Is* she, Rutter?'

Rutter only laughed.

21
EMPTY HOUSE

George and Polly saw Paula Bentley arrive at *Rostrum*, and a little more than an hour afterwards saw her leave it. George knew why she had gone, of course, and also knew that she had told Noel a very different reason. As far as Noel was concerned, she had gone because she knew he was a friend of Gertrude Ryall's and, she had declared with passion, she wanted to clear her brother's name.

George telephoned her at the *Norfolk Hotel*, a little later.

'He was pleasant enough,' said Paula Bentley, quietly. 'I learned nothing from him, I am afraid, unless—'

'Yes,' said George, hopefully.

'I thought he showed great interest in my story about Miss Dalton,' said Paula. 'In fact I am sure that he did, although it may not mean a great deal. Mr. Loftus told me that if you wanted me to do anything else, you would tell me.'

'I will,' said George. 'There's nothing now. Thanks very much.'

He rang off, and looked at Polly, who maintained a remarkable calm. Nothing, thought George, looking at her and feeling a now familiar tug at his heart, was going to ruffle Polly very easily.

'Mr. Noel is interested in Pretty Polly,' he said.

'Seriously?' asked Polly.

'Yes. And Paula Bentley made sure that the interest was well maintained,' said George; 'she had what I call a confident voice. Odd thing—do you know whom she reminded me of?'

'No,' said Polly, 'I'm not a member of the Department yet, I can't read other people's thoughts.'

'That was a bit sharp,' said George, looking at her reproachfully. 'Oh, well, she reminded me of Bruce Hammond. Odd, as I said. Well, now, it's time we went out again. You know, don't you, that you can still—'

'Do I have to tell you *again* that I don't want to back out of this now?' demanded Polly. There was a sharp note in her voice, and George, who only a few moments before had been reflecting that it would take a lot to unsettle her, saw that she was finding it hard to maintain her composure. That was nothing to be surprised about.

'Oke!' he said, brightly. 'Well, there we are. All aboard for the kidnapping!'

'Supposing nothing happens?' asked Polly, in a low voice.

'Let's not suppose anything of the kind,' said George.

In the past few days, he and Polly had visited most parts of Bournemouth and many places on the outskirts. The most attractive feature of the town, according to their mutual judgment, was the number of open spaces, the mingling of the rural with the urban. There were, for instance, in the chines, places where one could imagine oneself in the heart of the country, yet be within easy distance of houses, shops and the sea. There was also, near *Rostrum*, Meyrick Park and the golf course.

A little after seven o'clock, George and Polly reached the

road which ran through the park and Polly, a little out of breath, climbed the steep path which led to the edge of the golf course.

Trees surrounded the course, and there were no houses in sight.

There were not many people about, perhaps because it was early evening.

Yes, it was very quiet.

George led the way from the short grass of the course towards a thick patch of trees, where the grass grew long.

He had seen two men who had been near them since they had left *The Pines*. There was nothing at all remarkable about the two men. They were dressed in grey flannels and wore no ties and, in fact, they were sunburned and looked as if they were too tired to walk far. That listlessness was deceptive.

Now and again there were other men in sight. The Errols, for instance, were carrying golf-clubs. Mark was the better player, and Mike was complaining most of the time. Hoffmann, in his guise of a middle-aged Jewess, was sitting on a wooden seat, 'her' coat flung open, face red from the sun, a cigarette dangling from 'her' lips. Now and again 'she' took off a shoe, and rubbed 'her' foot.

Dunster had lost his curls; his hair was cut short and his face dyed brown, and he looked as if he had two front teeth missing. On the art of disguise there was little that the Department needed telling, although the members used it rarely, and then only sparingly. Dunster passed within a few yards of Polly several times, yet was not recognized.

Polly and George sat on the grass beneath the trees, hidden from all but close observers. George, flushed and rather embarrassed, made many tentative attempts to turn the conversation into romantic channels, and was blandly repulsed. It was a game which he would not have minded so much if he had not felt that Polly was enjoying it. In some ways she appeared to him rather a mysterious wench.

A chauffeur walked past them.

It was not a place where one would expect to find a chauffeur in uniform—until he began scratching in the long grass with the end of a putter; apparently he was looking for a golf ball. He was of medium height, thick-set, red-faced. He did not look like Arnold Rutter, except when he glanced sideways at Polly and George, and George saw his expression.

George turned suddenly to one side, and said:

'Polly, seriously, I'm *not* such a fool as I pretend. I mean, hang it...' he went on at some length, and when the chauffeur was out of sight, he said in a whisper: *'That was Rutter!'*

Polly's heart leapt. 'Are—are you sure?'

'Quite sure,' said George. He stood up, and added restlessly, 'I'll be back in a few moments, Polly!' He smiled and waved at her, and went on to the course. Hoffmann was now sitting on the grass with his back against a tree, nursing his feet. As he passed him, George whispered out of the side of his mouth:

'See the chauffeur? That was Rutter.'

Hoffmann gave no sign that he had heard the words, but soon afterwards the Errols came near, and Dunster was passing. They all saw his hands moving with bewildering speed, and the news spread.

'Rutter is dressed as a chauffeur. Rutter a chauffeur.'

Meanwhile Polly, left alone, lay back on the grass under a tree and closed her eyes, saying with some vexation:

'Why *must* he be serious?'

She murmured like that from time to time, but her heart was beating fast, and little noises in the grass made her start. She tried not to allow anyone who might be watching to notice it. She wondered if it had been too obvious, if George ought to have stayed—and then she felt something prick into her arm. It made her jump and sit upright. She turned her head, but saw no one near. As she rubbed her arm and saw a tiny globule of blood, she felt an excitement and a fear so great that her throat was constricted and her head swam.

A man came from behind the tree.

Polly began to feel overwhelmingly sleepy.

The room was dark.

Polly opened her eyes, and realized that. Her head was aching, but not enough to worry her. Her mouth was dry, but she felt no pain except in her head. Cautiously, she moved her arms; she was not bound. She moved her legs and, after a few minutes, stood up.

There was no light anywhere, and there was no sound.

She stood quite still, listening, bewildered—and very frightened. She thought she heard a faint thumping noise, and after a while realized that it was the thumping of her heart. Then she heard a scratching sound. It reminded her vividly of the moment when she had gone to her room to write a letter, before she knew that George was anything more than an inane ass. The noise continued, and there was no break in the darkness. She shivered, although it was not cold.

There was a different sound, the scampering of tiny feet on boards. Something brushed against her foot and she screamed: 'No!'

Then there was silence.

The 'something' had been a rat. She stood stiff with fear, with her hands resting on the arms of the chair.

A board squeaked outside.

She could not see the door, only the light which shone under the bottom of it, but she heard a squeaking sound, and guessed that the handle was turning. She tried to compose herself. When the door was flung open her lips were set and her eyes narrowed.

A bright light filled the room.

It shone on her and she closed her eyes against the glare, trying to repress a sob of fear. She was conscious of the light, against which her eyelids seemed a faint red, of voices, of a man's footsteps. Then a man gripped her arm, roughly, and a cloth was thrown over her head. It was heavy, dusty, close. She started to struggle, to try to throw it off, but hardly had she started before she stopped and went quite still. She must not give way to panic, she must not, she must not...

She prayed.

A man's fingers were tight about her arm.

'Come with me,' he said.

He led the way up the stairs, still pulling at her arm. She tried to hurry, and slipped twice, but he gave her no respite, and at last she reached the top, breathless, the blood pounding through her ears.

'Come *on!*' her companion growled, and slapped her bottom.

Fear, the nearness of panic and the unsteadiness of her limb faded, not completely, but partly swallowed up in a surge of almost petulant anger. The spanking was an indignity! Unconsciously she lifted her chin and set her lips. She made herself walk more steadily; she found to her intense satisfaction that she could do that, that she was now less frightened.

'In there,' the man said, and he pushed her forward. She sensed that he was going to slap her again, and she flung out her arm as he released it, aiming high. She struck his face, and made him gasp. Then she snatched off the cloth, as she entered the room.

It was empty but for one man—Rutter. She saw him really

clearly for the first time. He was in the chauffeur's uniform, but however he disguised his face he could not disguise his eyes. Then she realized, with a shock, that he was *not* disguised; his skin was fresher, his face less stiff; this was the real man, he had been made up before.

'Go and see the man,' said Rutter. 'Bring him up in twenty minutes.'

Her warder, at whom she glanced swiftly, was one of the nondescript fellows with baggy flannels, crumpled collar and soiled shirt—one of the men she had seen on the golf course, perhaps the man who had plunged the hypodermic needle into her arm. He went out and closed the door softly.

Rutter did not move; only his lips had moved slightly when he had spoken. He seemed intent on quelling her spirit with his gaze, and absurdly, it made her want to laugh. Of all the unreal things and people she had met, this man was the most unreal. Only his 'go and see the man'—probably George—had made her alarmed, and even that alarm faded. She was pleased with herself, yet at the back of her mind there was the knowledge that her courage was a brittle thing which might break at any moment. She licked her lips, and realized that she was thirsty. Near by was a hand-basin, and a tap was dripping.

She wished Rutter would speak.

After a long, unnerving pause, he did so.

'Have you ever dealt with Hubert Bentley?' he asked.

She was so startled that her 'no' came involuntarily, and she was angry with herself, she should have refused to answer at first, and then said yes. Rutter seemed satisfied that 'no' was the truth, but the truth shook him. There was a long pause before he asked another question.

'How many of George's friends are in Bournemouth?'

'About—about ten,' she said.

'Is Loftus here?'

'He—he wasn't.'

'Craigie?'

'He—he was in London this afternoon.'

This was all right; she had been told to tell the truth except on certain points, and she knew them off by heart. It was a help, because the man obviously believed her, and it was good that he had started with questions which she could answer truthfully—except about Bentley. He did not look away from her, as he asked:

'Did Loftus send Paula Bentley to Bournemouth?'

'Paula—' she began, and then raised her hands, as if taken completely by surprise. 'Bentley! *His* sister.'

'Yes,' said Rutter. 'Did Loftus send her to London?'

'I don't know,' she said, and her words were barely audible. 'I don't know, I knew about her brother.'

'What did you know about him?'

'That—that he sold some papers, I don't know what papers—*I tell you I don't know!*' she screamed, for he just looked at her, and now she found it more difficult to resist the compulsion of his gaze.

'Is Loftus still interested in Noel?' he asked.

She hesitated, and darted a glance towards the door. She saw a fresh expression on his face—he looked pleased, and he asked again in a softer voice:

'*Is* he still interested in Noel?'

'*Yes!*' she cried. 'Yes, yes, he—'

'Go on,' murmured Rutter. 'You are doing very well, Miss Dalton, don't spoil it now.'

She said: 'He believes Noel is—is a criminal, he believes Noel is—is responsible for all that happened, but—'

'Go *on*,' repeated Rutter.

She cried: 'I can't go on, I won't answer you!' She turned and rushed towards the door. He stepped swiftly forward, gripped her wrist, and twisted her arm so that pain shot up from the wrist to her elbow and beyond, and she caught her breath. He flung her away from him, and said:

'You will answer. What does Loftus think of Noel?'

'He—he thinks he is a—' She paused, and then added in an agonized voice: 'I can't go on, I can't...'

'You must go on,' said Rutter. He walked towards her, looking at her steadily all the time. He took her wrist and began to twist, and she did not know that pain could be so great—until, when she remained silent, he took her little finger and bent it back.

She cried: 'Don't, *don't*! I can't stand it. I can't stand it!' Her eyes were filled with tears of pain, she did not know how she managed to maintain any pretence. Her finger seemed red-hot. George had warned her that this might happen, she knew that she must withstand enough pressure to make her 'admissions' seem plausible.

'Then tell me what Loftus thinks of Noel,' said Rutter.

'He thinks he is—a neo-Fascist,' she said, in a tremulous voice. 'He thinks he worked for the Nazis, that he is trying to avenge them, he thinks he might do great damage in the country.'

'Go on,' said Rutter, in the same level voice.

She said: 'He thinks that Noel worked against England throughout the war. He—the Department—knew there was someone. He thinks that Noel wants to make the—the Department a scapegoat, that's why he's worked like this, that's why he killed Mrs. Hammond, why he tried to kill Christine Loftus.'

'I see,' said Rutter. 'He is not a fool.'

'Is it—*true*?' she gasped.

'Not quite true,' said Rutter, and he laughed. 'What else do you know?'

She said: 'Not—not very much. There was a time when the Prime Minister backed up the Department, but—but the way Loftus and Craigie treated Noel altered that. All the men are—are in great distress.'

'They would be,' said Rutter. 'Yes, they would be.' He looked triumphant, and he was smiling when footsteps echoed outside, and there was a tap at the door. He called out, the door opened, and the nondescript-looking man pushed George into the room.

22

THE TRIUMPH OF GEORGE

George was in a bad way. His collar and tie were torn, his blackened eye was bleeding a little above the lid, and there was a rent in the knee of his trousers. He had his lips set tightly, he glared, he even tried to resist as he was pushed into the room.

He saw Polly.

He drew in his breath, took a step towards her, and perhaps would have reached her had the nondescript man not stopped him. He shook off the man's hand, but stood still, staring at Polly. There was despair in his eyes. Seeing him, Polly wondered if it were possible that Rutter could possibly suspect that most of this was put on for his especial benefit.

The nondescript man closed the door, took an automatic from his pocket, and stood on guard.

George said: 'Polly, have they—hurt you?' His voice was thick.

'Not really hurt,' said Rutter, smoothly. 'She is nothing like so badly hurt as she will be if you are not wise, George. I want you to answer some questions.'

George looked at Polly, despairingly. She avoided his eyes; she was not really convinced that he was acting, and he looked as if he had been through worse torment than she.

Rutter asked:

'How many of your colleagues are there in Bournemouth?'

'About—ten,' George said, in a voice that was so low that Rutter spoke sharply, and made him repeat it. The questions which he had asked Polly followed, and the answers, some reluctant, some flung at him defiantly, were all the same as hers. Rutter went into greater detail, George gave more trouble in some ways and less in others than Polly, and as he answered he looked at her, with abject misery in his demeanour and in his colourless voice.

'Does Loftus propose to make any further attempt to prove what he thinks about Noel?' asked Rutter.

George said: 'He won't give up. It doesn't matter what happens to us, he won't give up, and *you* won't win.'

'Fine words,' said Rutter. He still looked delighted with himself. 'You are wrong. By this time tomorrow I doubt whether there will be such an organization as Department Z. It has taken a long time to break it, but—'

He checked himself, but George was still looking at Polly, and did not appear to hear what he said.

'You must be more precise,' said Rutter. 'What does Loftus plan tonight?'

George said: 'Damn you, I've said too much!'

'You have said so much that it would be a pity to spoil it now.'

George said nothing.

Rutter went to Polly's side, and took her wrist. She knew what was coming, and gasped even before he even touched her little finger. George made a movement towards her, but the nondescript little man pushed the gun forward, and

George stopped. The little finger was pressed back, not sharply, not even painfully; it was like a caress. Then he jerked it back, and a scream forced itself from Polly's lips.

George flung himself at Rutter, who had expected it and drove him back with a punch to the face. George staggered against the wall. Rutter motioned to the man with the gun, who took a pair of police handcuffs from his pocket. He dragged George to the wash-hand basin, and fastened one cuff about his wrist, the other about the towel-rail of the basin.

Polly shrank back.

'You must not blame me,' said Rutter. 'You must blame the obstinacy of your dear friend.' He looked at George. 'I am not pretending. I shall break every bone in her fingers if you are obstinate, and that need only be a beginning. Why don't you be sensible, George?'

George said: 'If you hurt her—' He broke off, but continued to stare at her. He stared for a long time. Then he began to talk in a low-pitched, monotonous voice. Loftus, he said, had decided to take a last chance. He no longer had the backing of the Home Office, and there was a likelihood that the police would be advised not to support him or the Department. Loftus was taking a chance on that. He had summoned every available agent, and there would be a raid on *Rostrum*— just before dawn. He had selected that hour, George said in reply to a question, because Noel was likely to be more easily frightened into confessing if he were woken up from a heavy sleep. No, Loftus had no further information, so far as he knew. Everything depended on making Noel speak. It would mean using pressure; Rutter ought to know what *that* meant. Yes, Loftus and Craigie as well as all the others knew that it was a desperate effort. It was their future against the success of the effort, and anything was worth trying. They were aware that if Noel did not talk, if he made a statement to the authorities of what had happened, it would probably mean a prison sentence for all who were involved, but…

George shrugged his shoulders, hopelessly.

'I think that is an *excellent* idea,' said Rutter, and he laughed. 'Well done, Loftus! The time was bound to come when you would go too far. Oh, *very* well done.' His laugh was almost a chortle. 'I can think of no better way of making sure that the Department never comes to life again—and a prison sentence! A fine reward for service.' He was speaking as if Loftus were in the room. 'I did not expect you to help me *quite* so freely, to play into my hands *quite* so foolishly. After so many years— this!' There was a glitter in his eyes, and George, watching him and pretending to show no interest in what he said, marvelled at the change in the man. He seemed exalted.

'Yes, Loftus may have his last fling,' said Rutter. 'I will let him wake Noel up, allow the inquiry to begin and when there is sufficient evidence to send Loftus and all of them to prison, then I will interfere. How pleased Noel will be when I rescue him! He will hardly pause to think that I might have warned him beforehand. *How* many men can Loftus call upon in all, George?'

George muttered: 'I think about twenty.'

'About twenty,' murmured Rutter. 'So the others are travelling to Bournemouth now. They will probably arrive on the seven-thirty from Waterloo. You were wise to tell me the truth. I know a great deal about the Department, you see. The number of its agents in this country is twenty-seven. Hammond and four others are not able to play a part in this. That is a pity, but there will be another way of dealing with them.'

George said: 'What—what are you going to do with— with us?'

Rutter said: 'I am going to leave you here together, until

the rest is over. Then I shall come back and I shall shoot you both—I will not make it a prolonged ordeal, you have earned some consideration. He made a motion to his man, who took from his pocket a small cardboard box; it was filled with wax. He went first to Polly, with one hand gripped her nose and made her open her mouth, then forced the wax in. When he released his fingers her mouth closed and she bit on the wax. It seemed to fill every part of her mouth, and she struggled for breath until her nose was clear. The man did the same to George, a listless, helpless George. That done, he released George from the basin, took some cord from his pocket and bound them both tightly then tied a scarf round their mouths. When it was finished and they were on the floor, on opposite sides of the room, Rutter looked at them, smiled serenely, and went out.

George looked across at Polly.

He could not move hands or body, but there was an expression in his eyes which gave her some reward, some solace, for what had happened. In George there was obviously a feeling of great triumph. She knew that he had lied to Rutter, that Rutter's acceptance of the story was all important.

It was a good thing that the same sense of triumph filled Rutter as he went downstairs.

Loftus reached *The Pines* by road a little after eleven o'clock. By then, the full company of the Department was present. Mark's wife had left, the maids had also gone, and there were only the men on duty. Many of them had arrived in Bournemouth on the late train, and had been seen and followed to *The Pines.*

Rutter received a report, confirming much that George had told him.

Loftus went into the small lounge—and Hoffmann, still dressed in woman's clothes, got up from a chair. Hoffmann's fingers moved at lightning speed. Loftus could not read the sign language, but Mike Errol translated. It was a curious conversation, tense and urgent.

Hoffmann spelt: 'I have seen George. I have left him bound and gagged, in case they go back to him. Rutter is to allow you to enter the house. Noel will not be warned. Rutter will interrupt when you have gone far enough with Noel to ensure a prison sentence.'

Mike translated, almost word by word.

'What time?' asked Loftus.

Hoffmann's fingers sped on their message.

'Just before dawn,' said Mike.

'Does Rutter think we are disowned by the police?'

'Yes.'

'How many men are we supposed to have?'

'Twenty.' The fingers went on moving. 'George arranged everything as his instructions said.'

'Good!' said Loftus. There was hopefulness in his bright eyes and in his manner. He turned to Mike, and asked:

'Has Carr been warned?'

'Yes. He suggested,' went on Mike, 'that it might be a good idea if he telephoned Noel and told him to let him know at once if he had any further trouble from you. That might get passed on to Rutter, and remove the last trace of doubt.'

'Good idea,' said Loftus, promptly. 'I'll give Carr a ring.' He did so, and Carr, as always, was eager to help.

Thus it was that Noel telephoned to the room beneath the house and told Rutter what Carr had said.

'A very thoughtful policeman,' said Rutter, slowly.

'Will you tell me what *you* expect?' demanded Noel.

'I expect Loftus to bring his men here, and I think I shall be able to deal with them,' said Rutter. 'Your men have arrived, and they have their instructions. I think you need have no worry tonight, Noel, Loftus will be dependent on his own men, and they...' he laughed. They will get many surprises!'

'I don't like the mystery,' said Noel.

'But there *is* no mystery,' Rutter assured him. 'It could not be better, my friend. Loftus will lead his men here on what amounts to a criminal attack, and they will be stopped before they get into the house. I shall not go to bed tonight. I will be there in person to superintend. I assure you that you need have no fears.'

'I hope you're right,' said Noel.

'I *am* right,' said Rutter.

Noel replaced the receiver, lit a cigarette and paced the study, nervous and on edge. Then, as he got his thoughts into good order, he began to smile. There was nothing of importance except the room below, even if Loftus broke in, and it was unlikely that he would even be able to open the strong-room door. The combination had been altered, and it was not a door that could be forced. He was foolish to have fears. The only two people who knew the truth were dead. Mattley's administration was toppling, Loftus, Craigie and the Department were about to make their swansong. What *could* go wrong? With police support, Craigie and Loftus could be dangerous, but without it...

Noel broke off in the middle of these thoughts, and put a telephone call through to London. A sleepy voice answered him—the voice of Joseph Witticome, Member of Parliament for a Midland Division. Witticome was not in the Government, but he liked it to be known that he had his ear close to the ground. He was a staunch supporter of Hemmingway

Noel, but he knew nothing of the truth of Noel's secret activities.

'Why, hallo, Noel!' he exclaimed, and sat up in bed with a jerk. Sleep faded completely. 'I'm delighted to hear from you—how are you?'

'I'm very well,' said Noel, and, after a while, admitted that he was worried. 'That infernal business the other day has upset me,' he said.

Witticome laughed. 'You mean with Craigie?'

'Yes,' said Noel.

'I shouldn't let *Craigie* get on your mind,' said Witticome, smugly, 'I told you the other day, I think he has had far too much rope—*far* too much. He certainly won't have any more. I have it on the best authority that Mattley has ordered the Department to cease its activities until after the debate tomorrow—and believe me, it won't start up again! Why, it will be one of the biggest scandals of the century! The Department has had far too much power, *far* too much. Mattley, I believe, is going to throw the blame on Craigie for acting without authority, but that won't save Mattley. Nothing can save either of them.'

'I'm very glad to hear it,' said Noel, and he nearly laughed into the telephone. 'Thank you, Witticome. I feel much easier in my mind—it is not pleasant to feel that one might be visited by a party of foolish young men.'

'If you have any trouble from Craigie,' said Witticome, 'just send for the police. *They've* had instructions.'

Noel thanked him again, and rang off; he laughed with relief as soon as the receiver was replaced.

Witticome could not get to sleep for some time. He was very pleased indeed. Noel was a man worth having as a friend. What a fortunate thing, thought Witticome, that he had spoken to the Under-Secretary of the Home Office that evening—how *very* fortunate.

It did not occur to him that the Under-Secretary knew that he had Noel's ear, and had elaborated the story with great delight—after a request, tantamount to instructions, which had come from Number 10.

Outside *Rostrum*, in the early hours of the next morning, Loftus, the Errols, Hoffmann and Bannister stood in the porch. Other men were hidden by the trees, fully aware of the nearness of Rutter's men, watching them, though apparently oblivious of their presence. Loftus talked in a whisper which travelled far enough for his purpose.

He gave clear instructions.

He and his small party would break in. Once they were in, a supporting party of five would take possession of the ground floor, and two more men would go upstairs to look after the staff. The rest would stay at vantage points in the garden. He exhorted them all to take the greatest care, for this was their last chance and if they failed—but then, said Loftus, they must not fail.

At half-past four he began to work on the lock of the front door. At a quarter to five, he and the first party went in. The house was silent, nothing stirred outside except the leaves in a slight breeze. When they got to the first floor Loftus stationed the Errols and Bannister near the study, and took Hoffmann with him to look into the other rooms.

The two men detailed to look after the servants came up and went to the second floor—and there they walked into the ambush which was prepared for them. Chloroform pads were used, effectively, quietly.

The five men who were to watch the ground floor also fell easy victims to Rutter's men.

One by one the Department agents in the grounds were attacked and overcome. There was little noise—everything went with remarkable smoothness, a success so complete that Rutter, when the reports reached him, had a momentary feeling of doubt. He rapidly dismissed it. Of course it was easy, Loftus was not prepared for such a carefully prepared trap.

In the meantime Loftus had found Noel's room, and stepped inside. The Errols and Bannister followed him, and Hoffmann went in last and closed the door. They moved so silently that Noel did not wake up until Loftus put a hand on his shoulder.

23

THE PROFESSOR WITH NINE LIVES

Noel opened his eyes, saw Loftus, hitched himself up in his bed and gaped. Loftus's face was hard and set. Only a bedside lamp was on. The other men stood back in the shadows; as far as Noel could see, Loftus and he were the only people in the room.

He said: 'Lo-Loftus!' and his voice was shrill.

'Yes,' said Loftus. 'Here again, Noel, and this time I am not going away without results.'

'You—you can't—'

'I can and will go to any lengths to make you tell the truth,' said Loftus. 'Where did you get the T.N.25 formula?'

He had not intended to start with that question; the fact that he did proved that it was uppermost in his mind. It did not greatly matter how he started, however, for Noel was not likely to regain his composure easily; the hour had been well chosen. Loftus even forgot the careful set-up, the trap so elaborately set to counter Rutter's trap; he even forgot that it did not greatly matter whether Noel talked or not. All he wanted was to get Noel and Rutter together, and Rutter would come, surely there could be no doubt of that.

'I—I don't understand you,' Noel gasped.

He tried to sit up, and Loftus pushed him down again. At the same time the Errols moved forward and stood motionless at the foot of the luxurious double bed. Their faces just showed in the dim light.

'Where did you get the formula?' repeated Loftus.

'I—I don't know what you mean! What formula? Loftus, if you don't go, I—I'll send—'

His voice trailed off, for Loftus clenched his fist and thrust it towards his face. Noel was so frightened that for the first time Loftus discovered one truth about him. There was no courage in Hemmingway Noel.

Loftus said: 'Listen to me, Noel. You are in this business so deep that nothing will ever get you out. You employ Rutter. You are responsible for the death of Dr. Morritz, for the death and injuries of the people in Alum Chine, for the death of my man Grey on the cliff—they are your direct responsibilities, and there is much more. Treason—betrayal—murder. Before I leave tonight I shall know everything.'

Noel gasped. 'There isn't anything to know, I've told you the truth.'

Loftus struck him on the side of the face, not heavily, but hard enough to send his head back on the pillows and to make him lie there, staring up, quite demoralized.

Where did you get the formula?' demanded Loftus.

Noel gasped. 'Rutter got it!'

'When?'

'Months ago, months ago! I refused to do business with him, he wanted to sell it to me, I referred him to the Government, I know nothing else—'

Loftus believed part of what he said: Rutter himself had

obtained the formula. The most important thing was that Noel admitted acquaintance with the man.

It was hard to believe that Rutter was probably within earshot, that the door of the dressing-room might open at any moment. Surely he *was* there.

'You know a great deal more,' said Loftus. 'How long did you work for Germany?'

'That—that is a lie!'

He broke off again, for the Errols moved forward. He was about to scream, but Loftus clapped a hand over his mouth. The Errols tore off his pyjama jacket, and then raised him up. Mike took a length of cord from his pocket, and as Noel sat shivering he tied his wrists to the bed-posts. He sat there, his chest bare, his face distorted—and then Loftus altered the position of the lamp, so that it shone directly on his victim.

He took out a knife.

Noel gasped: 'What—what is that? What—*Loftus!*' His voice was a scream. 'Loftus, you can't torture me, you can't.'

'I shall do whatever I think necessary to make you tell the truth,' said Loftus. His face, so grim and set, his eyes, glittering in the subdued light, seemed to petrify Noel, who stared as the knife flashed, and winced when it moved towards him.

'*Loftus!*'

Then the ceiling light went on.

Had Loftus not been expecting it, had there been no plot within a plot, it would have taken them by surprise. As the light flashed on, the door of the dressing-room opened and armed men streamed in. The Errols backed away. Mike turned, as if to go to the door—and one of the men fired and brought him down with a flesh wound. He knocked against Hoffmann, who went sprawling. Mark stood quite still, while Loftus stared at Rutter, the knife still in his hand. Noel sat helpless, almost sobbing in terror.

'An interesting picture,' said Rutter, and raised his hand.

A vivid flashlight made them blink; there were three flashes in all, and with each a photograph was taken—of Loftus with the knife, and of Noel stretched out, with his chest bared.

'A *most* interesting picture,' said Rutter, and took the knife from Loftus. 'All right, Noel, you need not worry.' He motioned to one of his men, who cut Noel free as he went on: 'All your men outside have been dealt with, Loftus, as well as all those inside the house. None of them has been hurt, I assure you—not seriously hurt. All will be here when the police arrive, with all the forces they require. Wasn't it fortunate that Noel, suspecting something like this, planned to have friends here?'

Loftus said nothing.

'Have you *quite* lost your tongue?' sneered Rutter. 'I am not really surprised. I know your desperation; your friend George was good enough to tell me what you were planning to do.'

'*George!*' gasped Loftus.

'You under-estimated his regard for Miss Dalton,' said Rutter. 'Well, Loftus, you are caught red-handed, using methods more suited to a Gestapo officer than to an English-man. What a story it will make! I wonder what sentence you will get, Loftus? Ten years, perhaps—even more. You might have escaped with less if you had the authority of the Govern-ment, but you have none. How foolish! What a rash move you made tonight.'

Loftus stood still, and his eyes seemed aflame.

'You will, of course, tell the police that I was here,' said Rutter, 'but your evidence will be worth nothing—why should they believe you in your attempt to malign such an upright gentleman as Hemmingway Noel?' He laughed again. 'It is *perfect*, Loftus. I told George how kind it was of you to play like this into my hands, to make sure that you had no chance at all to defend yourself.'

Loftus said: 'You—*planned*—this.'

'As the culmination of years of striving and years of sacrifice,' said Rutter, and he told Loftus what he had told Noel, of his hatred for Craigie, for Mattley, for the Department, of his efforts and his plans. None of this concerned T.N.25. For once he enjoyed hearing himself talk; obviously he felt convinced that his wildest dreams had come true. He was drunk with triumph. And that robbed him of the sinister touch which had always sat so evilly upon him.

'So it is over, Loftus,' he said, slowly. 'You will not even have the satisfaction of knowing the truth of this. Your absurd suggestion that Noel worked for Germany over a period of years will be laughed at—and *should* be laughed at!'

Loftus seemed to flinch.

'You really thought it was true,' marvelled Rutter. 'Oh, the truth is far different. I wonder how much I can safely tell you?' He looked at Noel, who was lying back with his eyes fixed on Loftus, and added: 'You were *quite* wrong to attack Noel. He has been an unhappy victim of my scheming. He thought I was his friend, but I have no time for friends. One day, when you are in prison, you will understand what I have been doing, for whom I have been working. Perhaps it will be known before Mattley dies—unless he dies soon, now that power has been snatched from him.'

'It's not been taken away—yet,' Loftus said.

'It will soon be gone,' said Rutter, softly. 'That and all his grandiose ideas—but I must not tell you too much, Loftus. Perhaps it would be better left for you to imagine, to discover as each development becomes widely known. This I *can* tell you. The explosive which Noel was making was *not* T.N. 25. But then, I think he realized that. The samples he had here were of powerful explosives, but not the greatest one. Only Toller and Morritz had that. Do you remember the explosion at Alum Chine, Loftus? *That was caused by a thimbleful of T.N.25!* You see its possibilities?'

Still Loftus said nothing, and none of the others stirred.

Noel said: 'You—cheated—me.'

Rutter laughed. 'What a fool you are, Noel, when you are stripped of your absurd pose. Oh, it does not matter,' he went on, 'nothing said here will ever be believed by the police, or by anyone except Loftus and his few remaining friends. And yet— perhaps only Loftus had better hear.'

He turned to his men.

Loftus stood quite still. He saw Mike and Mark struck over the head and rendered unconscious, and Hoffmann treated in the same way. They did not resist. Rutter was looking at him all the time, and when it was finished, he said:

'No, *Noel*, I did not cheat you. I merely gave you an instalment of the real thing. Loftus has been tricked—Loftus and Mattley—Washington and Moscow. They all *think* they have the proper formula now. The second half was sent to Washington and Moscow yesterday. But compared with the *real* T.N.25 that formula is innocuous, not worth a moment's trouble.'

'Oh,' said Loftus, in an absurd voice.

'Oh,' mimicked Rutter. 'Surprised, Loftus?'

Loftus said: 'Er—no. No, not really surprised. So the real thing is still unknown, except to Toller.'

'The *only* man alive, besides myself, who has it,' said Rutter, 'and I will sell it in due course to Noel and to others, and—'

'Well, well!' said Loftus, stupidly. 'Of course. I was quite blind, Rutter.'

Rutter looked at him sharply.

'Quite blind,' repeated Loftus. He shrugged his shoulders

helplessly, and as if in self-reproach. 'I should have understood before. I wonder if you wanted me to learn what I know now?'

Rutter said: 'Be careful, Loftus.'

Loftus snapped: 'What good will carefulness do now? What chance have I of overcoming the prejudice that this will create? What matters if you kill me because I have learned too much? That might be better,' he went on more slowly. 'Yes, I think it would be. *Only* you and Toller know the formula, Rutter. So—*you must have obtained it from Gabriel Toller!* Freely given, I suppose? He was dealing with you while working for the Government. No wonder he escaped each time you attacked him! The Professor with nine lives!'

And Loftus laughed.

'The Professor with nine lives! Well done, Rutter! It is very nearly perfect. Not once—not *once*—did we suspect that the real Gabriel Toller was working with you.'

Rutter said: 'You know now.'

'Oh yes! And one day he will take another of his daily walks and get rid of his guards and join you, I suppose? You will have the formula, you can sell to each Government or any one you can select—or to a ring of manufacturers led by Noel here. Yes, it is clever, Rutter, far cleverer than I thought. You ought to be most pleased with yourself.'

'I *am* pleased,' said Rutter.

'Oh yes! Still, remember the old saw. Many a slip—' He laughed again, but not so loudly.

'There will be no slip now,' said Rutter.

'No? So you'll kill me after all? Well,' said Loftus, and he sounded as inane as George Henry George, 'who can blame you? They would investigate the circumstances of the attempts on Toller's life afresh, wouldn't they? That is, if I made my statement. It would not matter whether I were believed or not.'

Rutter said: 'Yes, Loftus, they would. You will never make that statement.'

'Odd thing,' said Loftus. 'George Henry George is bright, there's no doubt about that. He was always asking: why should a professor have nine lives? His favourite joke. I suppose you wouldn't like to let me know everything now? I mean, no harm could be done, could it?'

Rutter said: 'George and the girl won't live much longer than you.'

'Oh,' said Loftus. 'Poisoned? If not, they will live—they were to be taken away from the empty house at dawn. I knew you wouldn't be able to spare any men from here at dawn. A good time of day, dawn. Hark! There's a cock crowing!'

He raised a hand; and there was silence in the room, silence until he lowered his hand, then raised it again. A tiny glass phial hit the panel of the bed. As it did so a cloud of gas rose up, and Loftus swung round and crashed a fist into Rutter's face, then dropped to the floor. Three shots rang out; all of them missed him. The cloud grew thicker, and the men began to cough, including Loftus. They could not see because of the tears streaming from their eyes and the pain at their eyes and nose and throat—the pricking, burning pain caused by tear-gas.

As they struggled, as Rutter tried to clear his eyes enough to see where Loftus was, Superintendent Carr and a strong force of the local police led a raid on the house. Tear-gas was freely used downstairs, there was little serious opposition, and when Carr himself entered the bedroom, Loftus was as helpless with the tear-gas as any of them.

In spite of it Loftus was trying to laugh.

* * *

Craigie pressed the button beneath the green light in the mantelpiece, and Mattley came in. The Prime Minister's eyes were bright, and there was no winter in his smile. His cigarette stuck out at a jaunty angle, and he raised his hand in greeting.

'Hallo, Loftus! Are you all right?'

'All sound in wind and limb, sir,' said Loftus, now quite recovered.

'Have you got the whole story?'

'There's very little missing,' said Loftus, 'and I think George will get the rest in time for you to include it when you wind up for the Government tonight. He is talking to Noel now.'

'What of this man Rutter?'

'I've done all the interrogating necessary with him,' said Loftus, in a grim voice. 'Do you remember, sir, in 1940 you gave evidence against a man court-martialled for cowardice under fire?'

Mattley hesitated, and then said slowly:

'Yes, I do remember something about it.'

'That was Rutter,' said Loftus. 'Hence his knife in you, sir. He had equally strong reasons for hating Craigie. Hate complex, but he is sane enough. When Rutter offered his services to Noel, he—save our blushes!—was convinced that he and Noel stood in greatest danger from the Department, and he set out on a deliberate attempt to smash the Department by every means in his power. The idea grew. You were known to favour international control of armaments, and Noel and Company did not like that a little bit, because of the strict limitation of profits and all that pertains. So they spread their arms and included the breaking of your administration in their pretty plot. That was incidental, of course. What they most wanted was Toller's explosive and a competitive world market. They knew he was working on T.N.25. Toller, as you know, once worked for Dakers. Dakers have a curious habit of not paying their research workers very well. Toller felt that he was being cheated of a just reward—and Rutter discovered that he was bitter about it. They talked. Rutter offered a large sum, knowing he could get financial support from Noel. Toller took the bribe, and then a formula was prepared and given to you, one which was not quite up to the full strength. Toller thus justified himself as a patriot— wonderful man, Toller! However, there was mystery as to how the formula reached other hands. Morritz was one possibility, and naturally we assumed that he had disclosed under threat of death. To make it look more realistic, Rutter arranged fake attacks on the Professor—and we swallowed that, sir, all of us swallowed that.'

'I certainly did,' said Mattley.

'And why not?' asked Loftus. 'I first began to wonder after the explosion at Alum Chine and the death of Morritz. Then there was another attack and a theft from Toller. You'll remember at the time that I suggested it was pointless.'

'Yes,' said Mattley.

'It was a mistake on Rutter's part,' said Loftus. 'He wanted us to believe that Toller was still in grave danger, and he elaborated it too much. Still, Toller might have been sitting pretty, with a little luck. Of course, we ourselves helped to make Toller seem quite genuine. We put up an Aunt Sally, and when we took an imaginary Toller to Bournemouth, Rutter saw his chance and used another dummy to spread further confusion. Very clever! Another pointer, had I chanced to see it, was that the man they put up—a disreputable actor named Kelly—had no instructions except to try to fool us. We were to believe that Rutter now had the real Toller—or rather,' he added, smoothing his hair, 'Rutter wanted us to think that *he* thought he had.'

'Yes, I follow you,' said Mattley, after a pause.

'There isn't much more,' said Loftus. 'I have no doubt at all that Noel's syndicate was most anxious to split the United Nations. It would not have suited them to have, a happy family, and so they tried the tricks with the formula, making each Government think it had the real thing, but all the time sitting pretty with Toller's real discovery.'

'Have you got that formula?' asked Mattley.

'No,' said Loftus. 'Nothing in this world will make Rutter give it up, but I think you'll get it from Toller. I'd rather like to try, sir.'

'You shall,' said Mattley. He smiled. 'I won't even try to say thanks, but if there are some obscure references to a small band of men working for a little-known Department, in the course of my speech this afternoon, you are at liberty to assume that I mean you—and the others, of course.' He looked at Craigie and laughed. 'Neither of us is finished yet, eh?'

Craigie laughed with him.

Mattley had not been out of the office for twenty minutes before the Bournemouth telephone rang, and George came on the line. A rather smug George who, when Loftus answered, asked:

'Why did the Professor have nine lives?'

'That's enough,' said Loftus, grinning. 'Have you finished with Noel?'

'Oh, it was wonderful,' said George. 'He almost cried in his eagerness to blame everyone but himself. I've the names of all the people with whom he worked—nine combines in all, only two of them English, I'm glad to say.'

'Let's have them,' said Loftus.

'Right!' said George, and talked earnestly for ten minutes. The list of names was imposing. That finished, he said brightly: 'And after that I think I deserve a holiday, William.'

'For as long as you like,' said Loftus. 'I suppose you don't mean a honeymoon?'

'I do *not*,' said George. 'Er—not yet, anyhow. Wish me luck. Good-bye! Oh, Loftus! Loftus, are you still there?'

'Yes,' said Loftus.

'There's a curious thing,' said George. 'Nothing sinister, just curious. We found a pile of papers about Bentley at *Rostrum*, including some photographs of Bentley, his sister and her husband.'

'Well?' said Loftus.

'That husband,' said George, in a slow voice. 'Remarkable, William, it really is. I thought at first I was looking at a photograph of Bruce Hammond. A really striking likeness, there really is. Odd, isn't it?'

'Yes,' said Loftus. 'Is there anything else?'

'Talk about little Oliver!' said George, and rang off.

Loftus looked across at Craigie, who had been listening in on the other telephone and making notes. Craigie looked up with a curious smile, and Loftus said:

'Paula Bentley's often at Bruce's nursing home, isn't she?'

'Yes,' said Craigie.

'Without jumping my fences,' said Loftus, 'I wonder if she *could* put Hammond on his feet again? And Paula, for that matter. I—but confound it, we've got to get that list typed for Mattley!'

George and Polly sat in the small lounge, with the radio on. A few of the others were also there, including Bannister and Hoffmann—who had remembered, now, where he had seen Maurice. More came in, until the room was almost full. Superintendent Carr arrived just before six o'clock, and had time to tell them that every man who had been arrested at *Rostrum* was an employee of Noel's, employed to act on any instructions. Carr admitted being astonished. Such barefaced gangsterdom, in England, under the auspices of a public man like Noel!

George grinned across at the Superintendent.

'Nothing surprising in that, policeman! Lots of strong-arm men about, glad to do anything for a spot of the necessary.'

'Hush!' exclaimed Polly.

The six pips of the Greenwich time signal came over the radio, and silence fell upon the room—a portentous silence, as if the announcer knew that a vast number of people was waiting for the report of that fateful debate in the House of Commons.

He began to speak.

'In the House of Commons this afternoon, the Government received a complete endorsement of its policy, the censure motion moved by Mr. Lloyd Lovell being defeated by 387 votes to 9. Contrary to custom, the Prime Minister intervened in the middle of the debate, reading to the House a statement which, he said, he had just received from the leader of a small Department working on Government service, a Department whose members are few but whose work cannot be assessed or praised too highly. The statement which followed...'

'Polly,' whispered George.

'Polly!' He was alarmed as he looked at her.

'Quiet!' said Bannister, annoyed.

'Polly!' whispered George. He got up and went to her. She was sitting back with her eyes closed and tears streaming down her face. He held her hand. She clutched his fingers tightly. Then she opened her eyes and asked in a muffled voice for a handkerchief.

Later, they walked through the gardens, near the Pavilion, where man had trained nature and created beauty enough to make all who looked upon the flowers and the shrubs, in their glorious raiment, stare with wonder. But they were not looking at the flowers, nor at the stream passing through the gardens, where children still played. They were looking at each other.

'I *am* a fool,' said Polly. 'Crying!'

'Great Scott!' said George. 'I was delighted! Confound it, you would have been inhuman if you hadn't cracked sooner or later. You were—well, one day I'll tell you what I think of you, Pretty Polly!'

'George, supposing we'd lost? What would have happened?'

George looked surprised.

'Well, ask yourself. Now all will be friendship and joy among the nations, where there would have been deep hostility and suspicion. A little gang of men, respected men, deliberately planning to sabotage unity for the sake of filthy lucre: that's the truth, reduced to its simplest form. The astonishing thing is that they got away with so much, and dared do so much openly. However, why think of what might have happened? Noel and his boy friends will have their teeth drawn, Rutter and his will hang. Mattley, in the fullness of time, will hand over to the next administration, but it will be a smooth job, done in all friendliness. In fact this show will do more than most to lessen the tension among the political parties. Damn it, they *are* all doing what they think best! Oh, there are a few who support sectional interests, but at the core it's sound. All of which,' added George, 'is needlessly portentous. Look!' He leaned forward and took from her hair a playing-card. 'Short of combs?' he inquired.

'Fool!' she said, half laughing.

'It's time for fooling,' said George. 'I can't be for ever serious. Er—Polly.'

'Yes.'

'Will you marry me?'

Pretty Polly stood still, looked at him round-eyed, pink and plump and quite delicious.

'*Are* you serious?' she demanded.

'Never more so! I know being married to me might be a bit of a trial, but—Polly!' he cried, for her eyes were glowing, and in front of a hundred people and a number of interested children, he kissed her.

'You might,' said Polly, a few moments later, 'have waited until I *said* yes.'

ABOUT THE AUTHOR

John Creasey, born in 1908, was a paramount English crime and science fiction writer who used myriad pseudonyms for more than six hundred novels. He founded the UK Crime Writers' Association in 1953. In 1962, his book *Gideon's Fire* received the Edgar Award for Best Novel from the Mystery Writers of America. Many of the characters featured in Creasey's titles became popular, including George Gideon of Scotland Yard, who was the basis for a subsequent television series and film. Creasey died in Salisbury, UK, in 1973.

DEPARTMENT Z

FROM OPEN ROAD MEDIA

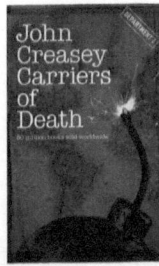

OPEN ROAD

INTEGRATED MEDIA

Find a full list of our authors and
titles at www.openroadmedia.com

FOLLOW US
@OpenRoadMedia

www.ingramcontent.com/pod-product-compliance
Lightning Source LLC
Chambersburg PA
CBHW031945010726
47493CB00007B/2082